Sherlock Holmes
Takes the Case:
Eight Tales of Mystery and
Intrigue

David MacGregor

Edited by David Marcum

First edition published in 2025
© Copyright 2025 David MacGregor

Hardcover ISBN 978-1-80424-624-5
Paperback ISBN 978-1-80424-625-2
ePub ISBN 978-1-80424-626-9
PDF ISBN 978-1-80424-627-6

MX Publishing, 335 Princess Park Manor, Royal Drive,
London, N11 3GX
www.mxpublishing.com

Cover design by Awan

Contents:

Introduction   1

The Adventure of the Alexandrian Scroll   5

Death at Simpson's   32

The Adventure of Peter the Painter   58

The Amateur Mendicant Society   86

Death of a Mudlark   111

The Adventure of the Scottish Coffins   133

Murder in Grasmere   156

The Adventure of the Mysterious Benefactor   183

Introduction

I have always enjoyed mysteries, beginning with the "can you solve it?" stories of Encyclopedia Brown and then moving on to the adventures of The Three Investigators, a series of juvenile fiction that had the imprimatur of Alfred Hitchcock himself. For some reason, the tales of the Hardy Boys never appealed to me all that much, but as I grew older, I found myself wading deeper and deeper into the depths of murder, master criminals, and nefarious deeds of all kinds.

There was the amazing output of Agatha Christie, the locked room puzzles of John Dickson Carr, the hard-boiled wizardry of Dashiell Hammett and Raymond Chandler, and any number of critical books and essays that sought to explain and dissect this genre of fiction that was dismissed by so many of the literati, most famously Edmund Wilson in his derisory articles published in *The New Yorker* in the 1940s. I feel fairly certain that the wise members of Monty Python would dismiss Mr. Wilson as a "silly person," and so did I, continuing to enjoy the Dover reprints of classic mystery stories, as well as novels by Charles Dickens and Wilkie Collins that contained some form of puzzle or crime.

However, standing above and beyond all of these authors and their works was a single volume, bound in crimson cloth, obtained at a Bag Day Book Sale, where you could purchase a brown paper grocery bag for one dollar and fill it with as many books as you could make fit. This was, of course, *The Complete Sherlock Holmes*, a book to rival any other text published since Johannes Gensfleisch zur Laden zum Gutenberg invented the printing press in the 15th century. Sherlock Holmes, to put it simply, was my kind of hero. The sad fact of the matter is that many famous heroes, both fictional and historical, were little more than sociopathic mass murderers, from Achilles and

Hercules to Genghis Khan and Napoleon Bonaparte. I could never understand the appeal of these somewhat ludicrous characters. How could anyone possibly admire or want to emulate any of them? For me, they were ridiculous, pathetic men (yep, always men) who were idolized in books written by more ridiculous, pathetic men who for some reason glorified these hopelessly maladjusted bringers of misery and death.

In contrast, Sherlock Holmes had zero interest in power, money, titles, conquests, or murderous exploits of any kind. All that he desired was to use his exceptional talents to help people, whether it might be a Duke or a governess. And beyond merely solving crimes, it was often Holmes himself who decided what might constitute justice. Then as now, the judicial system was rife with inequality and weighted heavily in favor of the wealthy and influential. Given that, Holmes (and the agreeable Dr. Watson) quite happily allowed thieves and murderers to go free in the interest of a greater form of justice. Ultimately, Sherlock Holmes was a kind of refuge compared to a real world that was often baffling, maddening, and manifestly unfair.

After graduating from college, I got the idea into my head to try my hand at a couple of mystery short stories and found a sympathetic reader in Charles E. Fritch, editor of *Mike Shayne Mystery Magazine*. One of those stories was a Sherlock Holmes pastiche, and I feel fairly certain the fact that the magazine went out of business the year after my story was published had little to do with my efforts. For the record, I count being published in a pulp magazine, having my writing publicly burned, and being hanged in effigy as a kind of Triple Crown of writing.

I then stepped away from mystery writing to turn my attentions to other endeavors, one of which was playwriting, and I was fortunate enough to find an artistic home at The Purple Rose Theatre in Chelsea, MI. After having a few plays produced there, I thought it would be fun to write a Sherlock Holmes play, and concocted a mystery/comedy/romance entitled *Sherlock Holmes and the Adventure of the Elusive Ear*.

The success of that play led to a sequel, *Sherlock Holmes and the Adventure of the Fallen Soufflé*, and then a third effort, *Sherlock Holmes and the Adventure of the Ghost Machine*. Happily enough, all three plays went on to be published by Theatrical Rights Worldwide (TRW) and have had productions from Texas to New Zealand. It was between the second and third play that the Covid-19 pandemic hit, and with theatres shut down, I got the notion into my head to adapt all three plays into novels.

Compared to a novel, a playscript is rather sparse when it comes to the total number of words, since it focuses almost entirely on the dialogue of the characters. Pretty clearly, more comprehensive descriptions and relating the inner thoughts of Watson would need to be added. Knowing that Conan Doyle had written four Sherlock Holmes novels, I settled on a length that would be shorter than *The Hound of the Baskervilles* and *The Valley of Fear*, but longer than *A Study in Scarlet* and *The Sign of the Four*. These three adaptations were subsequently brought out as individual paperbacks by MX Publishing, and also collected in a hardcover entitled *Sherlock in Love: The Holmes-Adler Mysteries*, then translated into Italian for Mondadori Publishing. On a bit of a Sherlockian roll, MX Publishing was also kind enough to publish my two-volume nonfiction book, *Sherlock Holmes: The Hero with a Thousand Faces*, which was an effort to account for the sustained popularity of the character over three centuries.

Somewhere in the midst of all this, I became aware of the MX Publishing anthology series of *New Sherlock Holmes Stories*, with all royalties going to the Undershaw School for children with learning disabilities (Undershaw, located in Surrey, was once the home of Arthur Conan Doyle). This good cause appealed to me, but then I was faced with the daunting challenge of trying to write a Canonical Sherlock Holmes pastiche; that is, a story that might have been written by Conan Doyle himself. This was no easy task, because I am, by nature, of a whimsical, absurdist, and often contrarian state of mind. Still, I enjoy a literary challenge, and I knew that I could count on the indefatigable editor of the series, David Marcum, to help wrench my tales into the Procrustean bed of a faithful Sherlock Holmes story.

Ultimately, I wrote seven stories for this series, all of which are contained within this volume. I discovered, to my own amusement, that much like Conan Doyle himself, I found myself drawn to writing stories in which Holmes and Watson not only investigate and solve the crimes, they then act as judge and jury as well. It's much more satisfying than the real world, in which the wealthy and powerful are rarely held to account for their tsunami of crimes and misdeeds.

Many thanks for picking up this slim volume, and I wish you happy reading!

David MacGregor
Howell, MI, 2025

The Adventure of the
Alexandrian Scroll

One of the greatest unsolved crimes of antiquity was the brutal murder of the brilliant Hypatia of Alexandria in 415 AD. Famed as a teacher, Neoplatonist philosopher, astronomer, and mathematician, she found herself bitterly resented by the early Christian Fathers of the Church, who were anxious to put all heathens and women in their place. When a mysterious scroll describing the details of her death appears and then suddenly disappears, Holmes and Watson are called in to try and solve this centuries-old homicide.

It was in the early days of my association with Sherlock Holmes that I began to get an inkling of how his moods would shift with the seasons. This had nothing to do with changes in the temperature or the weather itself. Rather, it reflected the kinds of clients who would appear on our doorstep asking for help. So it was that on an unseasonably warm day in late April that a steady stream of visitors had worn down Holmes's patience to a nub. In they came, one after another, men and women of all ages, and all with the same complaint – namely, they had been unfortunate enough to suffer the attentions of a pickpocket. Certainly the loss of a wallet or bracelet was no doubt dismaying, but what all of these prospective clients failed to appreciate was that Holmes's formidable talents were quite helpless in the face of this particular crime.

Even now, Holmes was at our window, gazing down at the throngs in Baker Street and shaking his head.

"Look at them, Watson. Bustling to-and-fro with no particular destination. Simply happy to be out and enjoying the sun, heedless to the fact that they are surrounded by predators."

"That's a bit of an exaggeration," I replied. "I realise that the nature of your profession has given you a somewhat dim view of humanity, but you make it sound as if we're little better than animals in the jungle."

"Worse than animals in the jungle. Far worse. Animals have only one purpose when they prey upon one another, but there is no end to the various horrors that human beings inflict upon both strangers and those they claim to love." Holmes paused and took a puff on his cherry-wood pipe, which I was quickly coming to associate with his more disputatious moods. "Ah well, it's a good thing you aren't out there, my friend. You would be relieved of your wallet within ten minutes and then be back here bleating at me for help."

"Ridiculous!" I retorted. "I'm not some callow young gentleman with his head in the clouds. And believe me, I know a pickpocket when I see one, and I would certainly notice a hand in my pocket."

"Really?" Holmes turned to me. "Prove it."

"Prove what?"

"I feel reasonably certain that I have spotted a pickpocket out in the street. Come here and see if you can spot him. Or her."

"Very well."

Standing up, I made my way to the window as Holmes moved aside and then maneuvered me for the best view along the length of Baker Street.

"You have one minute," said Holmes as he settled himself into his chair. "Describe the pickpocket in detail and I shall let you know if I concur with your judgment."

Looking down at the sea of humanity beneath me, I instantly despaired of the task at hand. The warm day had apparently brought out everyone in London, with many of the younger people wearing some striking piece of clothing with which they no doubt hoped to attract the attention of other young people. A scarlet handkerchief spilling out of a breast pocket here, a blue bonnet accentuating blonde curls there. This

6

was easily attributable to an entirely different sort of predatory behaviour than the kind Holmes had in mind, but one just as ancient and just as primal.

"Who could it be?" asked Holmes as he gazed at the ceiling. "Man? Woman? Young? Old? A lean individual as opposed to someone of a more stout constitution, thereby making it easier to slip through the crowd? Any candidates yet, Watson?"

Leaning closer to the window, I did my best to somehow see what Holmes had seen and deduce what he had deduced, but realised that in all likelihood I would simply make a fool of myself with a guess that Holmes would quickly puncture.

"Very well," I began as I turned back to Holmes, "I'm not going to pretend that my observational skills are remotely equal to yours. However, I assure you that I am quite capable of walking the streets of London without getting my pocket picked."

"A bold claim," returned Holmes. "In fact, you were out not too long ago fetching a newspaper. Are you quite certain you returned here with your wallet intact?"

"Come now," I was familiar with Holmes's needling when he was feeling bored, but this was a bit much. "I'll thank you for giving me a bit more credit than that."

Patting the pocket that contained my wallet for emphasis, I was instantly struck with pure panic. Reaching inside it, the absence of my wallet was all too evident. In the time-honoured fashion of anyone suffering such a loss, I instantly searched my remaining pockets in the vain hope that I had somehow inadvertently placed the wallet in one of them, but my frantic search came up empty as Holmes laughed at my discomfiture.

"Missing something, Watson?"

And then, as I stared at Holmes in my distress and embarrassment, I became aware that he was holding my wallet between two fingers.

"What the devil!" I cried. In two strides I had reached Holmes and plucked it from his hand. A brief inspection of its contents revealed that nothing was missing and I thrust the wallet back into my pocket with some vigour as Holmes smiled at me.

"Holmes," I began, pointing my finger at him, "that's unworthy of you!"

"Merely making a point," he answered. "A demonstration is so much more convincing than any explanation, don't you think?"

Still trying to catch up to the unnerving series of events that had just taken place, I finally realised what had happened.

"It was when you called me to the window and positioned me to look down the street. That's when you took it!"

Holmes inclined his head slightly, "I bow to your unparalleled deductive abilities."

Clearing my throat in a fashion that I hoped adequately communicated my irritation, I picked up my newspaper with the full intention of ignoring him for the next few minutes. The headlines on the front page were the usual assortment of government fiascos and European sabre-rattling, so I opened the paper, grateful for the opportunity to eliminate Holmes and his smug expression from my view. Halfway through an article on a new railway lane being constructed in the Lakes District, I became aware of the sound of Holmes drumming his fingers on the arm of his chair. Peeking over the top of my paper, I was dismayed to see that his dark mood had returned and that his gaze was fixed on a cabinet drawer that I knew contained a certain morocco leather case filled with dubious, if entirely legal, contents. I lowered the paper.

"Here we are, Holmes – It looks like we'll be able to take a train to Grasmere later this year. Won't that be nice?"

"Only if there's a murder in Grasmere," Holmes answered.

I turned another page. "And it would appear the British Museum has acquired some ancient scrolls from Egypt, courtesy of an expedition led by Lord Barwell."

"Why is it that thieving acquires a patina of respectability when it's done by the nobility?" enquired Holmes somewhat peevishly.

I hurriedly scrambled through some more pages for an entirely different topic and tried one last foray. "If the weather holds, do you fancy an outing tomorrow? It looks like England are playing Scotland at the Kennington Oval."

"Really, Watson. Rugby?" Holmes got up and strolled to the window. "Watching grown men knocking what little brains they have out of one another?"

At that, I finally concluded that anything I might say would quickly be returned to me with a good dose of cynical venom, and it was with more gratitude than usual that I heard the gentle rap of Mrs. Hudson against our door. Quickly moving to open it, I found her standing with a slight, pale man of about forty who was nervously twisting his hat in his hands. With his watery blue eyes and weak chin, he was the very picture of a man in complete and utter despair.

"A client for Mr. Holmes," announced Mrs. Hudson.

"Excellent!" I cried, with an enthusiasm that made Mrs. Hudson look at me in alarm. "Most excellent, indeed! Right this way, my good sir. Thank you, Mrs. Hudson!"

Closing the door, I ushered the gentleman further into the room, and was slightly dismayed to observe that Holmes hadn't even bothered to turn from the window.

"State your case," he announced in a bored drawl.

"My case?" The gentleman looked to me for guidance and I smiled in what I hoped was an encouraging fashion.

"Your reason for calling on Mr. Holmes. Are you being blackmailed, perhaps?" I suggested.

"Blackmailed? Oh no, sir. Nothing of the kind. It's a theft! A robbery!"

As my heart sank, Holmes turned from the window and cast a withering glare at our soon to be dismissed potential client. "Do tell. Wallet or pocket-watch?"

"Neither. It's a scroll, sir. An ancient scroll."

"Go on."

"My name is Norman Rashford, sir. I work at the British Museum in the Antiquities Department. We just received some Egyptian scrolls and I was given the job of cataloguing them, and now one of them has gone missing!"

"That's what I was just telling you about, Holmes," I interrupted, then turned to our guest. "Those would be the scrolls from Lord Barwell's expedition, yes?"

"Exactly, sir."

"Well, Mr. Rashford," began Holmes, "I am sorry indeed to hear of your loss, but a missing scroll no doubt relating to some kind of grain purchase or taxation issue doesn't particularly interest me. Beyond that, I have developed an intolerable headache. Watson will see you out."

With that, Holmes entered his bedroom and closed the door firmly behind him. I fully expected our visitor to meekly retreat back the way he came, but was surprised to see a spark of fire and anger in his eyes. Before I could say a word, he was at Holmes's bedroom door and banging on it insistently.

"Mr. Holmes! The scroll in question has nothing to do with grain or taxes. It's about a murder!"

Scarcely a heartbeat later, Holmes had opened the door and was peering at Mr. Rashford questioningly.

"A murder, you say?"

"Yes sir!"

"Very well. But why would I have any interest in a murder that took place in the ancient past? It isn't as if we can now bring the perpetrator to justice."

"No," returned our guest, "but you can bring the truth to light."

"Does the murder victim have a name?"

"Indeed she does, sir. Hypatia of Alexandria."

At this, Holmes's expression changed in a manner I had never before observed. Shock and excitement mingled in his

10

features as he spun Mr. Rashford around and directed him towards a chair.

"Sit. Sit, sit, sit. What do you require to tell your tale fully, Mr. Rashford? Tea? Coffee? Something stronger, perhaps?"

"Nothing at all, sir. I can see you have heard of Hypatia."

"Of course!"

Loath though I am to confess my ignorance in any situation, I realised that any ensuing conversation between Holmes and Mr. Rashford would be meaningless to me, as I had never heard of this person. Pulling out my notebook, I expressed this as diplomatically as I could.

"If you could just fill me in?"

"Hypatia of Alexandria, Watson!" he began. "Perhaps the most remarkable woman of her age. Certainly one of the most courageous and inspiring human beings to ever walk this planet. Philosopher, astronomer, and mathematician. There are those who claim that she was the librarian of the fabled Library of Alexandria, but that great temple of learning had already been destroyed before Hypatia was born. She was a famed Neoplatonist, and students flocked to her from all over the Mediterranean. And she was a great advocate of what she termed *apatheia* – that is, consciously endeavouring to remove all emotions and affections from her thought process in an effort to see and think as clearly as possible. She was murdered in cold blood in 415 A.D., yet no one was ever charged or accused of the crime."

At this, it became abundantly clear why Holmes held such reverence for this woman, as his own attitudes towards love and emotion of any kind mirrored hers almost exactly. Mr. Rashford, pleased to have found a fellow admirer in Holmes, added, "She founded her own school, lectured in both Plato and Aristotle, and according to the Syrian philosopher Damascius, was '*exceedingly beautiful and fair of form.*'"

"Indeed!" agreed Holmes. "She reputedly had many suitors, but rejected them all, prizing her own independence over any kind of security that a more domestic existence might provide."

"Or perhaps she was simply devoid of any kind of romantic inclinations," I offered.

"Unlikely," replied Holmes, "as she recommended playing or listening to music as a way to relieve lustful urges. The same remedy used by Pythagoras."

And as I cast my eye toward Holmes's violin in the corner, he continued, "She also utterly rejected Christianity, which at the time was becoming a more and more powerful political force as the Roman Empire crumbled."

"Bit of a rebel, then," I added.

"More than a bit, Watson. She enjoyed riding her personal chariot through the streets of Alexandria, no doubt earning the resentful and angry looks of men who felt that she didn't know her place. Perhaps most alarming of all, she advocated for the highest moral standards in politics, and publicly declared that politicians should act for the benefit of their fellow citizens."

"Remarkable," I muttered as I wrote all of these details down as quickly as I could manage. And to think that only moments earlier I had never heard of this woman. I looked from Holmes to Rashford. "So what happened to her? Do we know any details?"

"As a powerful and respected pagan woman," began Rashford, "the Christian leaders in Alexandria had no love for Hypatia and began a campaign of lies against her. While she herself hoped that the Neoplatonists and Christians could live together in peace, she was seen as a threat. While it was no secret that she was an unbeliever, she found herself accused of practicing magic and of being in league with evil. These efforts were led by Bishop Cyril, the Patriarch of Alexandria, who also expelled all of the Jews from the area in his attempt to create an entirely Christian city. Unfortunately for Cyril, all of his schemes to demonise and undermine Hypatia were in vain, because she was so well-known and beloved. So it came to pass that she was ultimately murdered, and as Mr. Holmes already related, her killing went unsolved. It goes down as one of the great mysteries of the ancient world and shocked the people of the Eastern Roman Empire, who subsequently came to regard Hypatia as a martyr of philosophy."

Holmes gazed at Rashford expectantly, until it became clear that he had said his piece. Holmes turned to me. "Allow me to fill in a few small gaps that Mr. Rashford omitted, no doubt with the intention of sparing your delicate sensibilities, my dear Watson. Hypatia was not merely killed, she was *destroyed*. One fine day in March, she was waylaid by a group of Christian men as she rode in her chariot. They dragged her into a building known as the Kaisarion. This was a pagan temple that had been converted into a Christian church by Bishop Cyril. She was stripped naked and then murdered with *ostraka*. In one of those delightful details that historians battle about far into the night, the word '*ostraka*' can be defined as either 'roof tiles' or 'oyster shells'. They gouged her eyes out, then tore her body into pieces and dragged her remains outside of Alexandria where they were set on fire, thereby symbolically purifying the city of her teachings and presence."

Approximately halfway through Holmes's recitation I had ceased to write in my notebook, utterly sickened by his description of Hypatia's unfortunate end. We sat in silence for a few moments, each of us wrapped up in our own thoughts, until Holmes finally spoke.

"It's one thing to read of these events in a history book. I am afraid, however, that I am afflicted with a condition that doesn't allow me the comfort of consigning such atrocities to the dim and distant past, for I know full well that similar events still occur on a regular basis all around the world. And when I think of Hypatia's last moments, when I think of her fear and horror at what was happening to her…"

13

Holmes trailed off with a small shake of his head, then turned to Rashford.

"This scroll. Tell me about it."

"It came along with perhaps four-dozen other scrolls," began Rashford, "all of them apparently belonging to one man who appears to have been a builder or architect in Alexandria. I began the rather painstaking task of cataloguing their contents, a process which was slower than I would have liked, owing to the fact that my proficiency in Greek lags behind my knowledge of Latin. As you surmised earlier, Mr. Holmes, the documents appeared to be related largely to the gentleman's business dealings, but just as I was about to stop work for the day and head home for dinner, my eye was caught by what was quite clearly the name '*Hypatia.*'"

Holmes's glittering eyes hadn't strayed from our client for an instant. "And knowing what I know of you, Mr. Rashford, I suspect that single word served to quicken your pulse."

"Indeed it did, sir," replied Rashford. "But I could see that it was a long document and my colleagues were already starting to file out for the day, and so I slipped the scroll inside my coat with the intention of studying it more closely when I got home."

"And were you able to do that?" enquired Holmes.

"Yes, sir. To the consternation of my wife, I ate a rather hurried dinner and then retired to my office to examine the scroll in detail. A short time later I was perhaps halfway through the document, and it was with some surprise that I looked up to see my wife entering my office and informing me that it was two in the morning, whereas I could have sworn that only a few minutes had passed since dinner."

"I am familiar with the phenomenon," nodded Holmes. "What were you able to learn?"

"That this man, this builder, had been present at the murder of Hypatia."

"So the scroll is a confession?" I hazarded.

"Not explicitly. He stopped short of implicating himself directly in the crime, but he was most certainly part of the mob and he witnessed the events. I had reached the point in the text where he was starting to explain the forces behind the conspiracy to kill Hypatia, and had just encountered the name of Bishop Cyril himself."

"Historians have always suspected his involvement," added Holmes, "and that he ordered her assassination, but there was never any proof. Given the fact that Cyril is considered to be one of the Church Fathers and a Doctor of the Church, it would be a considerable scandal and embarrassment were it to be revealed that he orchestrated the slaughter of Hypatia. Is that what the scroll alleges?"

"It does," returned Rashford, who then faltered. "At least, I believe it does. As I said, Greek is not my strongest language, and I was reading the text quickly as my excitement grew. But what I gathered was that Cyril had called a secret meeting of his most trusted associates to arrange for Hypatia's assassination. There was still a considerable amount of the scroll left to read, but as I stated, the hour was late and I had an early appointment this morning down at the docks to monitor another shipment from Lord Barwell's expedition. I left the scroll on my desk, fully intending to pick it up and take it with me when I returned to the Museum later today, but when I arrived home…"

As Rashford hesitated, tears welling up in his eyes, Holmes turned to me. "Watson, a brandy for Mr. Rashford, please."

"Of course." Moving to the sideboard and pouring a healthy snifter for our guest, I could see the poor man was almost overcome as Holmes regarded him solicitously.

"The scroll was gone," said Holmes as Rashford managed a nod. Holmes moved to the window, his grey eyes shifting back and forth in thought. "I assume you asked your wife about its whereabouts?"

Rashford nodded again as I delivered his brandy and he took a healthy gulp. "She knew nothing about it. It was my scroll and in my office. She has very little interest in my work at the Museum."

"I see," mused Holmes, "but when she entered your office in the wee hours of the morning to find you poring over the text, did you happen to relate its contents to her?"

"I believe I said a few words on the matter, yes," answered Rashford. "It was clear that I was in a state of some excitement, so I felt she deserved an explanation. But just as with Dr. Watson here, she had never heard of Hypatia, so she would hardly have any reason to take the document in my absence."

Holmes turned from the window and approached Rashford. "Then how would you account for its disappearance?"

"I don't know." Rashford drained the remainder of his brandy. "My only thought was that someone at the Museum or who was part of Lord Barwell's expedition knew of its contents. Needless to say, the translation and publication of a document attributing the murder of Hypatia to Bishop Cyril would be extremely embarrassing to not only the Roman Catholic Church, but the Church of England as well. It would be like revealing that John the Baptist had been the most noted murderer of his time. Given that, I expect that a pretty penny would be paid to keep the contents of the document secret. If the perpetrators of the crime searched my desk at the British Museum and found the scroll missing, then quite logically they would assume that I had taken it home with me. That's the only explanation I can offer."

"Then we must visit the location of this crime," declared Holmes. "I take it you have no objection, Mr. Rashford?"

"No, none. I'll escort you there myself."

"Excellent. Watson, come along. And bring your gun. We have no idea what manner of ne'er-do-wells we may encounter."

As we proceeded by cab to Upper Clapton and the home of our client, I brought out my notebook to fill in everything that I could remember of the conversation between Holmes and Rashford. In all my years of schooling I had never heard of this particularly sordid historical episode, and as I finished writing I looked across at Holmes.

"Is there anything else you think I should know about Hypatia or her death?"

"Just one minor point," answered Holmes. "If you're thinking of writing this up for your journals, you should know that Bishop Cyril is no longer referred to by that title."

"No?" I readied my pencil. "What is he known as now?"

"St. Cyril."

The remainder of our cab ride was spent in silence, with Holmes, Rashford, and I all looking out our respective windows, each wrapped in his own thoughts. Mine, I will confess, were of a particularly dismal hue as I pondered the dark history of our species, and it was with some measure of relief that I realised we were slowing to a halt. Upon descending from the cab, we approached the modest-yet-well-kept home of Mr. Rashford. Before we could enter, a dark-haired, rather handsome woman appeared in the doorway and regarded us questioningly, before turning her attention to our client.

"What's this, Norman? Shouldn't you be at the Museum?"

"Yes, of course, my dear," Rashford stammered out his response, "but the scroll I mentioned to you – I've engaged these gentlemen to aid in its recovery. Mr. Sherlock Holmes and Dr. John Watson, this is my wife, Eugenia."

As Holmes and I nodded our greeting, Mrs. Rashford cast a long and lingering look at Holmes, then stepped aside as we made our way into the house. Rashford led us straight to his office, and as we entered Holmes held up one finger.

"Please remain precisely where you are, Mr. Rashford. I need you out of the way for my investigation, but available for questions."

Bringing out my notebook, I took up a position near Rashford, who stood just inside the door. I was surprised to see that

Mrs. Rashford had followed us as well, apparently interested in observing the proceedings. As she watched Holmes, she kept one hand in a pocket of her dress and appeared to be unconsciously manipulating something inside it. Holmes began by simply scanning the room, his steepled fingers up to his lips as he took in every detail visible to the naked eye. He then proceeded carefully around the perimeter, stopping at the window and lifting it up. He turned to Rashford.

"Is this window typically latched?"

"Yes sir, but I opened it yesterday to get some fresh air in. I must have neglected to latch it in my excitement of examining the scroll."

Nodding at Rashford's explanation, Holmes brought out his magnifying lens and moved to the desk, surveying it in detail. There was a pen and inkbottle, a letter opener, a photo of a small child, and some scattered papers, but very little else. After a few moments, he pulled a small paper envelope from his coat and swept something I couldn't see into it. As if reading my mind, Holmes intoned, "Some small particles of parchment from the scroll, Watson. They may be of use if we find similar particles in another location." Pocketing the envelope, Holmes's gaze swept the room until it finally landed upon our client's wife.

"Mrs. Rashford," Holmes began, "might you possibly be able to shed any light on the disappearance of the scroll your husband brought home?"

"I'm afraid I have very little interest in old, dusty documents," she answered. "If you ask me, the modern world is more than interesting enough. Why waste time wallowing in the past when the present has so many marvels to offer?"

Out of the corner of my eye, I believe I caught Rashford wincing at his wife's remarks, but what I found striking was Mrs. Rashford's bearing and demeanour as she spoke to

Holmes. There was no hesitancy or hint of shyness in the presence of the detective. Instead, there was an almost challenging air as she regarded him with her striking green eyes.

"Quite," Holmes remarked as he turned back to the window, his eyes searching the street and the houses across from us. "Tell me, Mrs. Rashford, have you had any visitors today?"

"No, none." Hardly a second had passed before she caught herself. "No, actually Father Dawkins stopped by this morning. I missed Mass last Sunday due to a brief indisposition, and he kindly came by to see if I was feeling any better."

Still at the window, Holmes was almost unnaturally still, like a predator waiting for his unwary prey to stray into his path. "And did you happen to usher him into this office or show him the scroll?"

"Why should I do such a thing?"

Holmes turned to her with an enigmatic smile on his lips. "Why indeed?"

"And the scroll, Mr. Holmes? What do you imagine happened?" Mr. Rashford had remained rooted to the spot during Holmes's investigation, but now his anxiousness spilled out of him.

"I will be candid with you, sir," returned Holmes. "I believe you have seen the last of it, but we shall do what we can."

Stepping out of the house a few moments later without Rashford, Holmes inhaled deeply as he stared into the distance. "I fear we are in deep waters, Watson. Dark, fetid, almost bottomless waters." He paused, then regarded me with a sideways glance. "And yes, I agree with you. She is a most interesting woman. Particularly given the fact that she and her husband don't appear to be well-suited towards one another."

"Because of her lack of interest in his work?"

"There is that, and as we learned from her reference to Father Dawkins, she is a devout Catholic, and I suspect Mr. Rashford is not."

"What makes you say that?"

"I would draw your attention to the religious iconography in his office."

"I saw nothing of the kind," I admitted.

"Because there was nothing of the kind," explained Holmes, "even as his wife was unconsciously manipulating what I feel quite sure was a rosary in her pocket. Then there is the matter of the photo of the child on the desk."

"What about it?"

"I believe we happened on a not uncommon domestic tragedy. In the spring of youth, our fancies can be unduly invigorated by almost anything, and we may be swept up in a moment that we would subsequently wish to forget, unless that moment happens to result in the appearance of a child. At that point, the expectations of society and the responsibilities of parenthood can necessitate a joining of two people who are completely unsuited towards one another, both in temperament and faith."

"I see," I nodded, bringing out my notebook. "That makes perfect sense."

"The child in the photo was quite young," continued Holmes, "and given the ages of the Rashfords and the absence of more recent photos, I suspect that the child passed away some time ago, leaving Mr. and Mrs. Rashford to muddle aimlessly through the rest of their lives together until they tumble gratefully into their graves."

I paused to look at Holmes in shock, my pencil in midair. There was something positively inhuman in him at times, a quality that could be somewhat repellant, but no doubt aided him in his clear-eyed assessment of individuals and situations. Out of nowhere the bizarre thought came to me – Hypatia of Alexandria would be proud of him.

"By all means feel free to be appalled, Watson," remarked Holmes as he moved to examine the exterior of the window looking into Rashford's office, "for life and the actions of human beings are quite often appalling."

Crouching down, Holmes examined the ground beneath the window closely before standing back up. "Nothing. But the ground is so hard it would be difficult for any intruder to leave a trace. Now then, let's call upon the neighbours, shall we?"

Holmes walked across the street at a brisk pace and all I could do was trail in his wake with my brain still in a bit of a fog. Not thirty seconds later we were on the front step of the house just opposite the Rashfords.

"Would you like to see a front door opened in two seconds?" asked Holmes. And before I had time to reply he had rapped on the door with his cane and it had been immediately opened by an ancient, wizened woman who peered at us suspiciously.

"What do you want?"

"Ah, Madam! A very good day to you!" Holmes's eyes shone with friendliness as he smiled at the old crone ingratiatingly. "I am Mr. Hubert Weston and this is my partner, Mr. Oliver Crane, of Weston and Crane Architects. We have been commissioned to determine whether the spiritual needs of this neighbourhood are being adequately met by the number of churches in the area. You are a devout Catholic woman, I perceive."

"What?" The woman's eyes went wide. "How the devil do you know that?"

"The crucifix on the wall behind you suggests as much," replied Holmes. "Would you say that you and your neighbours are well served by Father Dawkins from – " Holmes turned to me. "What was the name of his church again, Oliver?"

In the time it took me to register that Holmes was addressing me by the pseudonym I had just been given, the old woman had shuffled further out on her porch to point down the street.

"St. Michael's, sir," she began, and once she started talking she seemed disinclined to stop. "Not three streets away. That's where Mrs. Rashford and I attend services. I noticed you were just over there to see her. Lovely woman. Bit of an unhappy marriage though, what with their little boy dying and all. It's a shame, really, but Father Dawkins is a wonderful priest and he's taken a special interest in Mrs. Rashford. He stops by to check on her three or four times a week."

"Excellent!" Holmes nodded his thanks. "Madam, you have been a veritable fount of information, and my colleague and I owe you our gratitude. This way, Oliver."

Once again chasing after the rapid stride of Holmes, I was struggling to understand precisely what was going on, a feeling no doubt exacerbated by the fact that I had found Holmes's instant ability to fashion new and plausible identities for both of us a little unnerving. When I finally caught up to him the best I could manage was, "What was that all about?"

"When I looked out of Mr. Rashford's office, I could see that old woman seated at her front window watching the street and instantly surmised that is where she spends the majority of her day. Who better to give us information on the comings and goings at the Rashfords?"

"Of course, yes," I managed, already a little out of breath. "And where are we going now?"

"To see the wonderful Father Dawkins," answered Holmes, as to my dismay he quickened his pace even further.

Scarcely two minutes later we were in St. Michael's Church, and with the instinct of a cat after a mouse, Holmes had unerringly made his way to Father Dawkins' office. Crossing the threshold a good five seconds after Holmes, I entered to see Father Dawkins seated at his desk and staring up at Holmes in shock. Before him was an open Bible, to which Holmes pointed.

"I believe you will find what you are looking for in the Book of Exodus, Father Dawkins," began Holmes. "The Eighth Commandment. Thou shalt not steal."

"What?" Father Dawkins' features were twisted in alarm and fear. "What's this about?"

"It is about theft, sir," returned Holmes. "It is about entering the home of a man you barely know, taking advantage of your relationship with his wife, and making off with a document from his office. In short, sir, I must ask you for the scroll you pilfered from Mr. Norman Rashford."

In his distress, Father Dawkins rose shakily to his feet, and I could see that in other circumstances he would be a rather handsome man, with his hair greying slightly at the temples and brown eyes that were no doubt kind and gentle as he listened to the hopes and fears of his parishioners. Now, however, as he swallowed nervously, a hard defiance came over his features.

"I don't have it!" he cried.

I would be hard pressed to adequately explain my actions at that moment, but with my blood up from chasing after Holmes and now reading the guilt-ridden expression of the man before us, I found my hand reaching into my pocket. A moment later, I was holding my revolver by my side. This was not lost on Father Dawkins, who instinctively raised his hands.

"I don't have it, I tell you! It isn't here! Go ahead, search my office! Search the church! Search every square inch of the grounds if you like! It isn't here!"

Looking for some explanation to Dawkins' rising terror, Holmes glanced back at me and spied the gun in my hand. A lightning flash of approval and amusement crossed his features before he turned back to Dawkins.

"You have been extraordinarily helpful, sir. Good day. And may God forgive you."

With a serendipity that I had come to take for granted, Holmes flagged down an empty cab scarcely ten seconds after we had exited the church, and we were soon clattering down cobblestones at high speed. Looking across at Holmes, I could see that his lips were pursed together in disapproval as he shook his head.

"It won't do, Watson," he began. "I'm growing soft in my old age."

"What do you mean?" I asked as I pulled out my notebook. "Have you deduced what happened to the scroll? Where are we going?"

Observing the pencil hovering over my notebook, Holmes raised his eyebrows as he looked at me. "Very well. In recognition of your armed assistance in a moment of crisis, I shall relate the series of events as I imagine they unfolded. First, as we have established, the union of Mr. and Mrs. Rashford is not a particularly happy one. As a good Catholic woman, this is something that she would have conveyed to Father Dawkins in the confessional or in the course of receiving his condolences for her deceased son. Concerned for her mental and spiritual well-being, he took it upon himself to call upon her on a regular basis, and I don't doubt that in due course his relationship with Mrs. Rashford took on a degree of familiarity that extends beyond that typical of a priest's interactions with his flock. This morning he arrived at the house while Mrs. Rashford was alone, and with the memory of her husband's excitement regarding the scroll fresh in her mind, she no doubt showed it to Father Dawkins."

"But she denied doing that!" I objected.

"No," returned Holmes. "You must train yourself to listen more carefully, Watson. I asked if she had shown Father Dawkins into her husband's office and she replied, 'Why should I do such a thing?' She never denied it."

"Quite right," I muttered as I jotted a note and could practically hear her words in my head.

"Having shown Father Dawkins the scroll, I suspect she explained its apparent importance as best she could, based on her limited knowledge. Perhaps this alone was enough to cause him alarm, or perhaps he has some proficiency in the Greek language, but either way he rapidly determined that the contents of the scroll could not be made public knowledge."

I was writing all of this down as rapidly as I could, but paused for a moment to look at Holmes.

"Then he did steal it! He must have! Holmes, I have never seen a more guilty man in my life."

"I concur, although whether he enlisted Mrs. Rashford as his confederate or returned to the house and made off with the scroll via the open office window I really couldn't say."

"Then what of his claim that he doesn't have it?"

"He doesn't. It's at this juncture that you must bear in mind the beautifully organised, yet inherently flawed, hierarchical structure of the system within which Father Dawkins lives and breathes – that is, the Roman Catholic Church. Stealing the scroll was one thing, but taking any further action would be inappropriate for a man in his relatively low position. And so – ?"

Holmes gazed at me expectantly and I was grateful when the obvious answer came sweeping over me.

"He's passed it on!" I cried. "He's given it to someone else!"

"Precisely," answered Holmes. "Which is why I fear I'm going soft. I should have recognised that immediately instead of wasting time dashing to St. Michael's to confront Father Dawkins. Ah, but here we are!"

With a scattering of gravel, the cab came to an abrupt halt as I looked out the window at the impressive sight of a massive Georgian manor house composed of limestone and accented with manicured topiary on both sides of an oak door through which an elephant could have passed.

As we exited the cab, Holmes answered my unasked question. "Behold the residence of Henry Edward Manning, better known as His Eminence, the Archbishop of Westminster and leader of the Catholic Church in England. We're about to make a call on him."

"What if he refuses to see us?"

"He won't. A man in his position is accustomed to being deferred to and will consider himself the master of every situation. And if, perchance, there are any obstacles to a private audience with His Eminence, I would remind you that you are a gentleman with a gun in your pocket, which will take precedence over any title or pretensions he may have. This way."

Following Holmes up the path towards the house, I reflected upon the fact that a day spent in the company of Sherlock Holmes always had the potential to lead in quite unexpected directions. It wasn't so long ago that I had been reading newspaper articles aloud in an effort to distract an irritable Holmes, and now I was faced with the imminent prospect of holding a gun on the Archbishop of Westminster with the aim of encouraging him to produce a stolen Egyptian scroll.

Happily enough, I was able to keep my gun in my pocket as we were immediately admitted into the house by an elderly butler who led us down a long, dim hallway towards the inner sanctum of His Eminence. Upon entering the cavernous room and observing the Archbishop of Westminster sitting behind an enormous mahogany desk, I instantly reconsidered my assessment of the butler as being elderly. Compared to the almost fossilised creature staring at us, the butler was little more than a spry young schoolboy. As the doors closed behind us, Holmes approached the desk and I remained where I was, staring at a gaunt, hatchet-faced man whose perpetually downturned mouth spoke of a lifetime spent issuing penance to the legions of sinners who had come before him.

"Your Eminence," began Holmes, "my name is Sherlock Holmes and this is my colleague Dr. Watson. I do hope you'll forgive this intrusion, but I have come to request the return of an Egyptian scroll recently stolen from the home of my client, Mr. Norman Rashford. If you would kindly hand it over, we will be on our way."

His eyes narrowing as he looked Holmes up and down, His Eminence finally spoke, "Are you accusing me of theft, Mr. Holmes?"

"Oh no, not at all," answered Holmes. "I apologise if you mistook my meaning. I am accusing you of receiving stolen goods from Father Dawkins, which is another matter entirely."

As Holmes spoke I began to move about the room, marvelling at an atmosphere right out of the Middle Ages. It was there in the rough stonework on the walls, the enormous wrought-iron chandelier, a profusion of lit candles, and a gargantuan fireplace that was currently dark.

"Mind you," Holmes continued, "possession of stolen goods is still a crime, but one I feel certain would never be prosecuted thanks to Your Eminence's exalted position. Nevertheless, I must still ask you for the scroll."

As Holmes held out his hand, the hint of an insolent smirk passed over His Eminence's features.

"I have no such thing in my possession. Good day, sir."

Nearing the huge fireplace, I became aware that while no flame was evident, there was most definitely residual heat emanating from it.

"Holmes," I said, "this fireplace is still warm."

Holmes quickly came towards me as the Archbishop rose from his chair to observe us. As Holmes verified my observation, he turned back to His Eminence.

"Curious that you would need a fire on such a mild day," remarked Holmes.

"I find that it helps to clear the damp from the room. No crime in that, I hope?"

Kneeling near the grate, I could see Holmes's eyes flashing over every inch of the fireplace, his nostrils flaring as he took in all of the information that his senses could provide. Pulling a small paper envelope from his coat, Holmes carefully swept some almost invisible particles into it as His Eminence tottered unsteadily towards us.

"What is it you're doing there?" he asked. "You have no right to remove anything from these premises."

"I shall be happy to let the courts decide that if you will," answered Holmes as he held up two small paper envelopes. "In this envelope I have some scraps of the missing scroll that I was able to salvage from the desk of Mr. Rashford. In this other envelope I have some unburned particles from the back of your fireplace. I feel confident that microscopic and chemical analysis will be able to confirm that the contents of both of these envelopes came from the same ancient manuscript."

His Eminence stared for a long moment, then shook his head at us. "There is nothing more pathetic than a very mediocre man who thinks he has done something clever. You are venturing into realms far beyond your domain, Mr. Holmes."

"Do tell," answered Holmes as he laid a steadying hand on my arm.

"Very well. Yes, Father Dawkins did come across the document in question. Not knowing what to make of it, he very sensibly brought it directly to me and informed me of its provenance. Having specialised in Classics at Oxford as a young man, I was able to read the Greek text quite easily and determined to my satisfaction that it was nothing more and nothing less than a scurrilous attack upon the character of St. Cyril. Knowing the inclination of the press and the public to make a sensation out of nothing, it was clear to me that burning the document would save considerable scandal and consternation, which is something that the Church doesn't need."

"So you admit it!" I cried.

"Do I admit destroying a heretical document? Yes, I admit that proudly and without reservation. And if you will check your history books, I think you will find that there is a long line of distinguished and revered men of faith before me who acted similarly. I am honoured to have been given the opportunity to join their company."

"And the cold-blooded murder of Hypatia of Alexandria," began Holmes, "that isn't something that troubles you in the least?"

"Who am I to question the wisdom of St. Cyril?" answered His Eminence. "The Church was not nearly so well established in his age as it is in our own, and Hypatia was clearly an obstacle to the spread of the faith. Cyril acted as he thought best, no doubt after much prayer and with the guidance of Our Lord."

As Holmes and I stood speechless, His Eminence spread his arms and looked upward.

"It is not for us to question or understand everything that transpires in this world. For those of us in positions to guide the faithful, what we offer are answers, hope, and the certainty that there is a better life beyond this one. Our holy duty is to smooth the path to God, not to ask troublesome questions or flaunt incendiary texts in the public arena. I fully understand that you gentlemen may not agree with the means, but I can assure you that the ends are well worth it. Good day to you."

Half-an-hour later, Holmes had still not said a single word as we walked slowly back towards the heart of London. He had eschewed any form of transportation, and I had kept my peace as I knew Holmes was utterly absorbed in his own thoughts. At length, however, I ventured the only question that had been preying upon my mind.

"Is there nothing we can do?"

"Nothing," answered Holmes. "Only two people read the document. One of them is an underling at the British Museum with a rudimentary knowledge of Greek, and the other is the Archbishop of Westminster, who studied Classics at Oxford. Who do you think would be believed?" Holmes paused, a sombre look in his eye. "But I will tell you this, Watson. A day of reckoning is coming for the Archbishop of Westminster and his kind. We may not be alive to see it, but the truth has a way of eventually worming its way to the surface, and it is then that all of the crimes and lies of the highest of the high will reveal them for the monsters that they truly are."

Two streets further on, Holmes paused to look around us. It was in truth a beautiful day, and London was suffused in the golden glow of the setting sun as myriads of people jostled around us heading home or to more festive assignations. Holmes, I knew, was oblivious to all this.

"So we would do well to consider our day. It began with a series of petty crimes that we were helpless to do anything about, and it ended with a conspiracy to keep hidden the details of one of the most infamous murders in history, which again, we are helpless to do anything about. I ask you then, as a professional consulting detective, what is the point of my existence?"

This wouldn't do. The last thing that I wanted was Holmes returning to Baker Street in such a dark frame of mind, and so I began talking, hoping for inspiration to strike as I continued.

"It's a lovely day, Holmes. In truth, the most pleasant day of the year so far. And do you see all of these people bustling through the streets? At any moment any one of them might appear in our rooms with a case. Nothing so simple as a pocket being picked, but a false accusation, a murder that has baffled Scotland Yard, or possibly a missing child. And they come to you as a last resort, as the one man in London who can somehow see light in the darkness, who can perceive order in chaos, and who can set the world aright. That is the point of your existence. Not to be omniscient and omnipotent, but to help those who can be helped when they have been abandoned by the rest of humanity. And so, if you will permit me, I have a proposition for you."

Holmes looked at me curiously. "I'm listening."

"Dinner at Simpson's. On me. We shall sit down, we shall dine sumptuously, and we shall drink a toast to Hypatia and to a world where truth and beauty do exist, and where the pursuit of both is the highest calling of mankind."

"Watson..." Holmes faltered, and I could see him endeavouring to master the emotions roiling within him. "I don't deserve you, my friend."

He extended his hand and I took it as we looked one another in the eye.

"Dinner at Simpson's it is," Holmes continued. "Although I have been thinking we should follow the good example of George Bernard Shaw and become vegetarians."

"Capital idea!" I agreed as we began walking again. "Let's discuss it over a jug of claret and a roast leg of lamb."

"With red currant jelly?"

"Elementary, my dear Holmes. Elementary."

Death at Simpson's

The venerable (yet now sadly defunct) Simpson's in the Strand restaurant was favored by Holmes and Watson for its famous roast meats, and was mentioned by name in both "The Illustrious Client" and "The Dying Detective." It was also favored by Arthur Conan Doyle, and in the 19th century was the favorite meeting place of Europe's most famous chess players. Distinguished by carving utensils with handles shaped in the form of chess pieces, when a carving knife finds its way into the back of a famously unpleasant English Lord, Holmes and Watson are called in to investigate a particularly savory crime.

I will confess, dear reader, that in an effort to tell this tale, I have endeavoured to begin it no less than a dozen times, but on each occasion found myself giving up less than a page into the narrative. I realise now that the hurdle I was unable to overcome was somehow finding the proper tone and moral stance, but if the story is to be told I shall simply have to make a clean breast of it and not concern myself with the wagging tongues of the public at large. The simple fact is that this case was easily the most enjoyable murder investigation that Holmes and I had ever embarked upon. I will go further to say that the murder itself wasn't nearly as gruesome as I anticipated, and the sheer tidiness of the affair made it easier to focus on the considerable charms of the location of the crime and the benefit rendered to the community. Finally, I should note that any persons whose reputations might potentially be sullied by the telling of this tale have passed into the Great Beyond.

But I fear that I am getting ahead of myself. Suffice to say, that on this chilly evening in early December, Holmes and I were quite happily ensconced at 221b Baker Street, with a gentle snow falling outside and a well-tended fire casting flickering shadows on the walls of our rooms. Holmes was utterly immersed in a chemical experiment of some kind, and I had sat down with the full intention of making some headway into Gibbon's *The Decline and Fall of the Roman Empire*. With a snifter of brandy at my elbow, I soon found my attention to the follies and foibles of the Roman emperors waning, as I descended into a not-at-all unpleasant fog reminiscing about a truly remarkable gingerbread cake that a grateful client of Holmes's had delivered only the day before.

How long I would have persisted in this reverie before dropping off into gentle slumber will have to remain a subject for speculation, as I dimly realized that Holmes had turned his attention from his flasks and tubes to our front door. Listening more closely now, I heard the gentle tread of footsteps on the stairs, and a moment later Mrs. Hudson had ushered Inspector Lestrade into our presence. Shaking the snowflakes from his hat and coat, he removed his gloves to hold his hands out to the fire as Holmes regarded him expectantly.

"Do help yourself to some brandy, Lestrade," began Holmes.

"You are very kind, Mr. Holmes," returned Lestrade, opening the decanter and pouring himself a healthy glass.

"It's scarcely the kind of weather in which one expects the criminal class to be unduly vigorous in their activities," continued Holmes. "In fact, I have often thought of devoting myself to a small monograph on the relationship between weather and crime. May I take it, then, that your visit is related to some crime of passion committed indoors?"

"Quite so," answered Lestrade. "And if you don't mind, I will relate the scant details of the case as I enjoy your quite exceptional brandy. After all, the body isn't going anywhere soon."

Holmes shot me an amused glance as I brought out my notebook. "Jot that down, Watson. Apparently, we are dealing with a non-migratory corpse."

Lestrade remained planted in front of the fire, but turned his back to it as he began recounting the events of the evening that had brought him to us. "Would either of you happen to be familiar with the gentleman known as Lord Percival Chesterfield?"

Holmes raised an eyebrow as I looked up from my notebook. "Watson may correct me if I'm mistaken," replied Holmes, "but neither of us has had occasion to make Lord Chesterfield's personal acquaintance. We are, however, familiar with the gentleman, and have had the misfortune of observing his public displays of poor behavior on more than one occasion. Do you happen to recall his temper tantrum at the British Museum regarding the general public disturbing his viewing of the Elgin Marbles?"

"Vividly," I muttered. "Absolutely disgraceful."

"Dr. Watson?" Lestrade turned in my direction. "I would be grateful for your candid impression." As I hesitated, Lestrade continued, "And you have my word that anything you say will never leave this room."

"Very well," I began. "To say that the man is an insufferable scoundrel scarcely scratches the surface of his utterly depraved nature. He is infamous for heaping abuse and the most vile language on almost anyone who crosses his path. He seems to thrive on the loathing of his fellow man, has sued more than one merchant into bankruptcy, and my understanding is that his wife killed herself rather than be forced to spend another night under the same roof as him."

"It was murder," interrupted Lestrade. "As sure as I'm standing here, he killed that poor woman in cold blood. Poisoned her with strychnine. The man killed his own wife with rat poison…" Lestrade's voice quavered and he took a moment to regain control of his emotions. "But Lord Chesterfield has influential friends in high places, and I was pointedly told by the Commissioner to drop my investigation."

"Didn't I read just last week that Lord Chesterfield is newly engaged?" I asked.

Lestrade nodded. "To the recently widowed Lady Pemberton, who inherited her husband's sizable estate. Presumably, Lord Chesterfield has found himself low on funds in order to support his various debaucheries, and so..." Lestrade trailed off, letting Holmes and me fill in for ourselves what dire fate might await the innocent Lady Pemberton.

"To put it bluntly," I said, "he's a madman whose title shields him from the consequences of his own actions. Why, Holmes and I once observed him spewing torrents of obscenities towards the staff at Simpson's simply because he noted a smudge on his water glass and because a napkin wasn't folded to his liking."

"You have captured the essence of the gentleman quite nicely," nodded Lestrade. "And, in fact, it was at Simpson's that Lord Chesterfield partook of his Last Supper, so to speak."

"You mean to say it's Lord Chesterfield who is dead?" I asked. "I assumed his temper had finally got the better of him and he took his rage out on some innocent bystander."

"Not at all," answered Lestrade. "The Lord himself was rapidly cooling to the touch when I left him."

"Dear, dear," muttered Holmes. "So it would appear that Lord Chesterfield has finally received his just desserts, as it were."

"He never made it as far as dessert," answered Lestrade with a puckish attempt at humour. "In fact, he never made it to his main course. And between us, good riddance. I'm heartily glad that the old curmudgeon is dead, because he has been a pain in my side on more than one occasion. If not for his title and money, he would have been rotting behind bars for the past decade. Still, murder is murder, so if you and Dr. Watson would care to accompany me, I would be happy to take you to the location of the crime."

"May I take it that his killer has not been apprehended?" enquired Holmes.

"Not yet."

"Do you have a suspect in mind?"

"None."

"You mean to tell us," I interrupted, "that a member of the British peerage can be murdered in the middle of a popular restaurant with no one the wiser?"

"It would appear so," answered Lestrade.

"And for this you propose to take Watson and me on a three-mile trek across London on a snowy evening? As you can see, we are perfectly happy where we are, and if the atmosphere of London is improved by Lord Chesterfield's untimely demise, why on earth should we stir ourselves?"

"An excellent point," returned Lestrade, "and one that I did consider, but there are other factors to be taken into consideration."

"Such as?" asked Holmes.

"For that, I'm afraid I must lay the blame at Dr. Watson's feet," answered Lestrade as he turned to me.

"Me?" I expostulated. "What on earth did I do?"

"Let's just say," continued Lestrade, "that if you had confined your interests to your medical duties, I wouldn't be here right now."

As my brow furrowed in thought, I caught the shadow of a smile crossing Holmes's face. "If I'm not mistaken, Watson, I believe our good friend Lestrade is referring to your literary efforts."

"What about them?" I answered, immediately on the defensive. "I have poured my heart and soul into those stories, and if I don't say so myself, managed to build up a substantial and loyal readership."

"And there is the problem, Dr. Watson," said Lestrade. "Your readers came to include several members of the Metropolitan Police. Most of them take the stories for what they are –

amusing, and perhaps occasionally instructive tales of mystery and intrigue. However…"

As Lestrade refilled his glass, I saw a look of apprehension cross Holmes's face.

"Oh no. You don't mean to say – ?"

"I'm afraid I do, Mr. Holmes."

"What?" I asked. "What's happened? What's going on?"

"Thanks to your dubious influence, Dr. Watson," Lestrade paused for a healthy swallow of brandy, "I now have two constables on the force who fancy themselves as new Sherlock Holmes-es: Constables Boswell and MacDuff by name. When I left them at the restaurant, I told them not to touch or move anything, and they were both crawling along the carpet looking for clues. They are determined to find the culprit by any means necessary, but I fear that any number of bystanders will suffer from their attentions."

Holmes shook his head. "So that in addition to defacing the crime scene, they are likely to charge some innocent soul with murder."

"I shudder to think who we will find clapped into darbies upon our arrival," said Lestrade, "but if I could impose upon you gentlemen to abandon your cosy abode, perhaps we can clarify matters as soon as possible."

"Well, well," Holmes pushed himself away from his chemical experiment. "Needs must, eh Watson? Let's make the best of it and enjoy a scenic drive through snowy London."

Five minutes later, Holmes, Lestrade, and I were headed in the direction of Covent Garden, and the drive was very pleasant indeed. The snow on the ground served to mute the harsh sound of horseshoes on cobblestones, and the luminous reach of the gas lamps was generously extended by the reflective qualities of the light snow that settled on every surface. Both carriages and pedestrians, mindful of slipping on slick surfaces, proceeded at a more cautious pace than normal, producing a kind of dreamlike vignette of a metropolis where time had slowed its inexorable pace. It was all rather beautiful, truth be told, and by the time we pulled up outside of Simpson's, all thoughts of a violent murder had drifted out of my mind.

As we descended from the carriage, I was swiftly brought back to reality by the cordon of constables holding back a sizable crowd that had somehow smelled the scent of noble blood being spilled the way vultures detect carrion from a distance. Better yet, a murder at Simpson's promised to be front page news because it was likely that some toff or other member of the so-called 'Upper Ten-Thousand' had met his demise. Holmes, Lestrade, and I entered the restaurant only to be met by more policemen, as well as a tall and rapier-thin *maître d'* whose typical air of sangfroid had utterly deserted him, given the events of the evening. He looked beseechingly at Lestrade, and then his gaze shifted to a seated waiter, who had the expression of a man already on the gallows, with his manacled hands twisting fitfully in his lap. He was middle-aged, with a swarthy complexion, and even at a distance I could see a fresh wound above his left eye.

"There's our man, sir." A large, bull-necked constable with bright blue eyes had materialized next to Lestrade. He was immediately joined by a shorter constable, whose thick black mustache served to almost completely obscure his thin lips. From this mustache came confirmation of the first constable's claim. "He done it, all right. Cold as ice, he was."

Swallowing down whatever his initial response might have been, Lestrade indicated Holmes and me. "Constable Boswell, Constable MacDuff. Allow me to introduce you to Sherlock Holmes and Dr. Watson."

I don't think either constable actually heard my name, as at the mention of Holmes their eyes had widened and both jaws had dropped. There then followed a stream of unintelligible gibberish from both that I could scarcely make out, although I believe the general gist of it was that they both revered and worshipped Holmes as if he were a living deity. Tempted as I was to point out that I was the person who had actually made Holmes famous, I kept my tongue as Holmes inclined his head at the two constables and then turned to Lestrade.

"If I might see the body, Inspector," said Holmes.

"Of course," answered Lestrade. "This way."

Exiting the lobby of the restaurant, we made our way to the gentleman's dining room, where tables draped with white table-cloths were ringed with light-brown wooden chairs, and comfortable booths upholstered in green leather lined the walls. Most of the tables were strewn with the remains of meals in various degrees of completion, as the well-heeled crowd had presumably fled for the exits at the discovery of the murder, and the management of Simpson's quite sensibly elected to leave the entire scene untouched until the arrival of the authorities. Near the entrance to the kitchen sat a spacious booth with curved seating, and slumped over the table was the form of a man with a large carving knife protruding from his back. This, then, was the late and unlamented Lord Chesterfield. I hasten to add that the highly distinctive handle of the carving knife was in the shape of a horse's head – or rather, a knight in chess, as Simpson's was the very epicentre of London's chess scene.

It was here that Englishman Howard Staunton had laid claim to being the greatest chess player in the world, and over the years such luminaries as the Austrian Wilhelm Steinitz, the German Emanuel Lasker, and the American prodigy Paul Morphy had crossed pawns. Upon the occasions when Holmes and I ventured to Simpson's for a meal, we would often see two grizzled heads ensconced in a booth and bent over a board. Speaking for myself, the appeal of the game paled in comparison to the sumptuous fare on offer at Simpson's, most especially their delicious roasts of meat that were carved tableside. I was chagrined to see that one of those roasts sat entirely untouched on a serving trolley next to Lord Chesterfield's table. Protruding from the roast was a large fork, whose handle was in the shape of a rook, thus complementing the knife lodged just to the right of His Lordship's spine. A single slice of beef had been cut halfway through, but then the carving knife had been used to much more deadly effect on Lord Chesterfield.

With his hands clasped behind his back, Holmes took in the scene of the murder from every angle, with Constables Boswell and MacDuff holding their breath to see if the great man himself might spy some clue that had somehow evaded them. Holmes inspected the body and the portion of the carving knife that could be seen, and then brought out his magnifying lens for a more detailed examination of the table itself and the serving trolley. The wooden ledge behind the booth received particularly close scrutiny, with both his nostrils flaring as he bent over to smell the wood. Diving beneath the table, Holmes emerged with a heavy glass pot which I recognized as the typical vessel used by Simpson's to hold their signature concoction of horseradish, and it was only then that I looked around to see that splashes of horseradish were on the serving trolley and the carpet as well. Holmes then beckoned towards me, and I was instantly by his side.

"What do you make of it, Watson?" he asked. "With a carving knife driven up to its handle into the back of the victim at that angle, what would be the cause of death?"

"Well, we can only be certain once a *post mortem* is conducted," I answered, "but were I to hazard a guess, I imagine that the blade sliced clean through the aorta. If you consider the position of the body, it would appear that death was almost instantaneous, and the absence of any blood emanating from the mouth or nose suggests that the blow didn't pass through the lungs."

"Excellent," nodded Holmes. "I concur with you completely. Whether the fatal blow was aided by sheer chance or a familiarity with human anatomy remains to be seen."

Holmes turned his gaze to the dining room and his eyes swept across it like the human panopticon that he was.

"Clearly, there were many diners here when the murder took place, but I will assume there were no witnesses."

"Quite right, Mr. Holmes," Lestrade looked suitably impressed. "How ever did you know that?"

"Given my knowledge of Lord Chesterfield and the condition of the roast next to his table, I suspect there was something that displeased him."

"Yes, yes!" It was the *maître d'* who now elbowed his way forward. "The kitchen had mistakenly included a pot of horseradish with his meal, which Lord Chesterfield positively loathed. He preferred a special tomato-based sauce, which our Chef prepared for him personally."

"And presumably," Holmes continued, "Lord Chesterfield let his displeasure be known at considerable volume."

"Yes, that is exactly what he did!" confirmed the *maître d'*. "In fact, he threw the horseradish at poor Georgios, his waiter, striking him just above the eye. Georgios, to his credit, immediately ran to the kitchen to correct this mistake. I accompanied him because Georgios has only been with us for a week, and I wanted to impress upon the Chef the importance of creating his signature sauce immediately."

"And how did Lord Chesterfield react to the disappearance of his server?"

The *maître d'* winced at the memory. "Not well. His shouts and curses were audible to everyone in the kitchen. He was furious – practically out of his mind with rage."

"Thus explaining the lack of witnesses to his murder," murmured Holmes.

"I'm not sure I understand," I said. "The *maître d'* and the waiter may have left the room, but there were still other guests seated at their tables."

"Indeed," nodded Holmes, "but I would impress upon you the importance of taking into account the habits of Londoners of a certain class. Had Lord Chesterfield been whispering something to a companion, almost every eye in the room would have been upon him. However, since he was bellowing his lungs out, every eye would have been studiously averted. The upper and middle-classes of England are a curious breed of *savants* when it comes to ignoring things they don't wish to see or acknowledge."

It was at this point that Constables Boswell and MacDuff, who had barely been able to contain themselves, interrupted Holmes's train of thought.

"And with no one watching him, that is precisely when Georgios came back into the dining room undetected and stabbed Lord Chesterfield!" announced Boswell.

"Why should he do such a thing?" asked Holmes.

Boswell and MacDuff looked at one another in mystification, perhaps recalculating their high opinion of Holmes.

"Surely it's obvious," began MacDuff. "He had been humiliated in front of everyone in the room – "

"And had just been violently struck with a heavy glass pot of horseradish – " continued Boswell.

"And his temperament simply couldn't take it," concluded MacDuff.

Holmes looked from MacDuff to Boswell with a bland smile.

"I see. And what is this 'temperament' of which you speak?"

"Well, he's a foreigner, sir," began MacDuff. "Fresh off the boat from Greece."

"It's the Mediterranean background," added Boswell helpfully. "They're a very hot-blooded people."

"Ah," Holmes nodded in comprehension. "Hot-blooded in the manner of Socrates, Plato, and Aristotle, you mean?"

Boswell and MacDuff exchanged an uncertain glance, giving Holmes an opportunity to deliver a short lecture.

"Gentlemen, if you wish to advance in your chosen profession, you would do well to clear your minds of any and all prejudices you may have concerning any race, ethnicity, profession, or gender. Human beings, each and every one of us, are capable of anything. Let the facts and the facts alone lead you where they may. In this case, Georgios, being newly arrived on these shores, would have been largely immune to Lord Chesterfield's colorful tirade due to his unfamiliarity with the language. Furthermore, were he of a homicidal disposition, he would most likely have killed Lord Chesterfield immediately after being hit by the pot of horseradish, because he quite literally had the knife in his hand at the moment he was struck. Instead, he put the knife down and accompanied the *maître d'* to the kitchen. Lestrade, you may release the prisoner. The poor man is no more guilty than you and I."

Here I will confess that while I had my notebook out, my attention has strayed to the untouched roast still sitting only feet away from the deceased Lord Chesterfield. It was a gorgeous thing as it sat on its silver platter, medium rare, with roasted potatoes nearby in a separate dish, and a flagon of brown gravy just waiting to be poured over them. The ever-vigilant Holmes took all this in with a single glance and turned to the profoundly grateful *maître d'*, whose colleague had just been cleared of all charges.

"I wouldn't wish to inconvenience you or any of the staff, but my friend Dr. Watson and I were just about to enjoy a late supper when we were called upon by Inspector Lestrade to come here to investigate the crime. I don't suppose – "

The effect of Holmes's words on the *maître d'* was absolutely electric. He thrust his chin into the air and cleared his throat. "Not another word, sir! It would be an honour to serve Mr. Sherlock Holmes and Dr. Watson as they consider the case. Please make yourselves comfortable!"

Holmes cast a bemused look my way, then turned to Lestrade. "Would you care to join us, Inspector? One can hardly do one's best work on an empty stomach."

"Capital idea!" enthused Lestrade. "Let me just clear the room so that we may focus on the case."

As Lestrade set about his task, Holmes strolled among the tables and booths, looking at each of them in turn before waving me towards him as he stood beside a booth not more than ten feet away from Lord Chesterfield's corpse.

"Let us convene here, Watson. This booth is free of any half-eaten meals which might distract you."

I was able to take Holmes's gentle jibe in good stride thanks to the knowledge that we were in the more than capable hands of the *maître d'* and his staff, who would no doubt exert themselves in an effort to keep Holmes and Lestrade happy and to somehow preserve the good name of Simpson's. As Holmes and I sat down opposite one another, the only object on the table was a chessboard with a game in progress, along with a single glass of red liquid. The chessboard and glass were closer to Holmes's side of the table than mine, and he proceeded to wave his hand over the glass and pronounced his verdict.

"Claret."

A moment later Lestrade had joined us, squeezing in next to me as Holmes took in the position on the board.

"Do either of you gentlemen play chess?" Holmes enquired.

"I'm afraid not," answered Lestrade. "A good game of chequers is enough to keep me happy. Although if it's a Christmas party, I must say I enjoy a round of Charades or Blind Man's Bluff."

"Watson?" Holmes flickered a glance at me.

"I know the rules," I answered, "but not much more than that. I certainly wouldn't be a challenge for any of the gentlemen who play here. What about you, Holmes?"

"My brother Mycroft and I played when we were children. Being older, he trounced me repeatedly, which gave him no end of pleasure. Until the day came when I decided that I didn't want to lose anymore."

"So you stopped playing?" I asked.

"On the contrary," replied Holmes. "Quite in secret and without Mycroft's knowledge, I studied up on the game for a solid month. In fact, a number of the games that I used to hone my skills were played right here at Simpson's. I became familiar with such strategies as The Queen's Gambit, The English Opening, and The King's Indian Defence, but I was especially drawn to the Ruy Lopez. It was developed by the Spanish priest Ruy López de Segura in the sixteenth century, fell into disrepute, then was rediscovered by the Russian Carl Jaenisch just a few decades ago. At the next opportunity I employed it against Mycroft, and with great satisfaction was soon able to pronounce '*Checkmate!*' – much to Mycroft's chagrin."

"And did you continue to beat him after that?" enquired Lestrade.

"Oh no," Holmes looked up as he noticed two serving trays being wheeled our way. "After that loss, I found that the chess set had been deposited into the rubbish bin. Mycroft refused to play me again. He accused me of cheating."

"How on earth were you cheating?" I asked.

"I was *trying*, my dear Watson. Trying harder than Mycroft was willing to try, and in his mind that constituted cheating. But enough talk of chess. I believe our food had arrived."

Sure enough, the *maître d'* and Georgios materialized pushing not one, but *two* serving carts, their contents covered by large silver lids concealing the salvers beneath them. Up close, I got a better look at the nasty wound sustained by Georgios, courtesy of Lord Chesterfield's pot of horseradish, but he had clearly insisted on staying on to serve the man who had just cleared him of all charges. In unison, they removed the silver lids from the salvers to reveal not one, but three different roasts, along with a dazzling array of side dishes. Close behind the *maître d'* and Georgios came the Chef himself, carrying two bottles of their best claret and three glasses. As he set the glasses down and began pouring the claret, he nodded to each of us in turn.

"Gentlemen, please accept this small offering on the house. What has happened here is absolutely dreadful and unprecedented in the history of the restaurant. You will have, of course, our full cooperation, and we would be grateful for any gestures that you might be able to extend to us, by way of preserving our reputation and clientele. Now then – " he turned his attention to the serving carts, " – what we have prepared for you are three different meats: A roast fore-quarter of lamb with mint sauce, roast sirloin of beef with Yorkshire pudding, and roast saddle of mutton with red currant jelly. We also have new roasted potatoes, baked beans, and vegetable marrow. Could I possibly interest you in some boiled neck of lamb with caper sauce or chicken Marengo? Perhaps some anchovies on toast or macaroni tomato? Our entire menu is yours for the asking."

"This is…" I found myself lost for words. "This is…*wonderful!*" Were those tears welling up in my eyes? I couldn't recall the last time that I was this blissfully happy.

"It looks absolutely splendid and is most gracious of you, Chef," said Holmes. "We will quite happily sample all of this fine fare as we discuss the case. Many thanks."

The Chef offered us a curt nod. "Then I will wish you *bon appétit.*" As the Chef made his way back to the kitchen, the *maître d'* and Georgios proceeded to pile our plates high with samples of everything from the serving carts. With no hesitation, Lestrade and I tucked in, while Holmes picked up a small piece of mutton, dabbed it with red currant jelly, and chewed thoughtfully as he analyzed the position on the chessboard.

I will freely avow that I am a man with a good appetite, but it was everything I could do to keep up with Lestrade, who appeared to be absolutely ravenous. I suspected his visits to Simpson's were far and few between on a policeman's salary, and he was determined to take advantage of the serendipitous circumstances surrounding this particular murder to their full extent. After doing significant damage to all three roasts, we proceeded to lay waste to a lemon jelly, a St. Clair pudding, and a truly

46

magnificent chocolate *blanc mange* and cream. Holmes, I was interested to observe, ordered only the *meringues glacé* and a cup of coffee for dessert. As he sipped it, he glanced across the table at Lestrade and me, who were both, admittedly, in a bit of a daze thanks to a surfeit of food and claret.

"Well, gentlemen," Holmes began. "You have dined as well as two Englishmen could ever hope to dine. Have you solved the crime?"

Gathering our muddled senses as best we could, Lestrade and I came back to the fact that we were seated just a few feet away from the corpse of Lord Chesterfield. As I turned in my seat, I could still see the gleaming silver knight at the end of the carving knife in his back.

"Suicide?" offered Lestrade, and for a brief moment I thought he was serious. Then I saw the smile on his face and began to laugh, which caused Lestrade to break out into laughter as well. This, in turn, caused my own amusement to increase, and within moments both Lestrade and I were quite helpless with mirth, tears running down our respective cheeks. Slowly, I became aware that the Chef, the *maître d'*, and Georgios had crept back into the dining room, but kept their distance. Across from us Holmes was simply shaking his head, although I could see that he was doing his best to suppress a smile.

"Elementary, my dear Lestrade!" I managed as I spooned the last morsel of pudding into my mouth. Toasting one another with the dregs in our claret glasses, Lestrade and I emptied them and turned our attention to Holmes.

"What do you make of it, Holmes?" I asked. "If it wasn't Georgios, who is our murderer? Where did he come from? And where did he go?"

"As to his identity, I confess myself at a temporary loss, although that will soon change. Where did he go? Out the front door. Where did he come from? Right here."

"Right where?" asked Lestrade. "We know he was in the restaurant."

"I mean right here," continued Holmes. "Where I'm sitting."

Lestrade and I looked at Holmes in bewilderment.

"How so?" asked Lestrade.

"The only evidence I can offer is circumstantial," began Holmes, "but I would ask you to consider the following. This wasn't a premeditated murder, as one would hardly choose Simpson's as the ideal location for such a crime. In addition, the choice of murder weapon, a carving knife, suggests the crime was of a spontaneous nature, with our murderer simply utilizing the best weapon within reach. Then there are the other tables as compared to this booth. Each and every one of them show evidence of at least two diners. There was only one diner in this booth. Indeed, he had not yet begun to dine. He had only a glass of claret and had pulled the board from the middle of the table towards him so that he could regard it more closely as he waited for his opponent and dining companion to arrive."

"That's all very well, Mr. Holmes," said Lestrade, "but how does that add up to murder?"

"Perhaps it doesn't," answered Holmes, "but let us continue our journey down this particular path." Holmes indicated the chessboard in front of us. "What we are looking at is a game in progress. Two gentlemen began the game, presumably earlier today, this week, or this month, but realized they wouldn't be able to finish it. Simpson's very kindly set the game aside until their return, so we can assume both gentlemen are regular customers. Our murderer sat where I'm sitting, playing the white pieces and puzzling over his next move."

"How do you know it was his move?" asked Lestrade.

"Because he is in check, Lestrade. His position isn't fatal, but it is dire. It would only be through the most delicate and sophisticated strategy that he would be able to extricate himself from this situation to try and manage a draw. Further, I would suggest to you that he is playing an opponent superior to himself, so that he is almost certain to lose."

"What makes you say his opponent is superior?" I asked.

"Our murderer is playing the white pieces, which afforded him the first move of the game. This could be mere chance, but you will note the missing black pawn in front of the queenside rook. This wasn't taken in the course of the game. No gentlemen, our murderer's opponent, confident in his ability, offered him pawn and first move to make the game more competitive. However, any advantage our murderer had was swiftly overwhelmed as white endeavored to play the Ruy Lopez, but then was confounded by what has come to be recognized as the Morphy Defence, played by black. Not knowing what to do, white blundered and fell into what is known as the Noah's Ark Trap, in which the white bishop is rendered helpless by the black pawns, thus leading to the position we see before us."

"That still doesn't add up to murder, Mr. Holmes," offered Lestrade.

"Doesn't it?" answered Holmes. "If I cast my mind back to my early games with Mycroft, all I remember is the anger and humiliation I felt after each thrashing. I knew that I was intelligent enough, but somehow the game negated any natural advantages I felt that I had. Time and again, it was like being wrapped in the coils of a constrictor until the very life was squeezed out of me. I was helpless, utterly incapable of eluding my grim ending. And here we have our murderer playing the white pieces, staring at what he realises is an almost inevitable fate. He considers one strategy after another, sips his claret, and feels the coils tightening. His pulse begins to increase as he grinds his teeth in frustration. He needs to focus every ounce of his concentration on the task at hand to have even the glimmer of a hope of success, and then…"

Holmes looked at me expectantly.

"Lord Chesterfield went off on one of his rants," I nodded.

"He flings the horseradish at Georgios," added Lestrade, "and when Georgios runs into the kitchen, His Lordship begins screaming and cursing at the top of his lungs, according to the *maître d'*."

"Everyone has their breaking point," offered Holmes. "Even the most respectable among us. I suspect the roots of this behaviour lie somewhere in our distant past, as outlined by Charles Darwin's evolutionary theories. When we are threatened or feel impossibly trapped, like a mother crocodile defending her nest of eggs against some predator, we lash out violently and murderously, with no thought of the possible consequences to ourselves. Simply put, the gossamer-thin thread of humanity in our chess-playing gentleman snapped, as it might snap in any of us given proper provocation. And there, only a few feet away, was a carving knife positively beckoning to him, for Georgios hadn't left it on the serving tray."

"No?" asked Lestrade. "Then where was it?"

"On the wooden ledge directly behind Lord Chesterfield, where Georgios had dropped it in his panic as he ran to the kitchen. If you would care to look, Lestrade, you will observe small drops of grease from the roast, as Georgios had already begun to carve it when he was assaulted by Lord Chesterfield. The knife was thus left behind, in full sight of our mystery diner who was sitting right here. It was a simple enough matter to stand up, take hold of the knife, plunge it between Lord Chesterfield's shoulder blades, then make his way out of the restaurant, with every eye averted."

"But...but..." Lestrade stammered, "If that's true, if there were no witnesses, then we can't prove anything."

"And it's here," began Holmes, "that we need to ask ourselves, do we really *want* to prove anything?"

Lestrade's eyes went wide. "Hold on now. Are you saying – ?"

"I'm saying that as a consulting detective, I am at perfect liberty to decide which cases I wish to pursue to their end. You, on the other hand, are an official representative of the police. I will leave it up to you to decide what your duties and conscience require."

A worried look entered Lestrade's eye as he considered what to do next. When the *maître d'* materialized beside us to enquire if we needed anything else, Lestrade straightened his shoulders and looked the *maître d'* in the eye.

"There is one thing I would appreciate knowing," began Lestrade. "Do you happen to recall who was sitting in this booth prior to the attack on Lord Chesterfield?"

"Of course!" the *maître d'* nodded. "It was Dr. Saxonhouse, waiting for his opponent, Dr. Halley. They both practice at Charing Cross Hospital and often stop here for some dinner and chess."

Holmes turned to me, "You're our resident physician, Watson. Are you by chance familiar with either of those gentlemen?"

"I consulted with Dr. Saxonhouse on one occasion and found him remarkably erudite and helpful," I answered. "I believe he also teaches anatomy courses at King's College. He's a tremendously accomplished surgeon, and is known for offering his services free of charge to the indigent. In fact, I believe he is on the short list for a knighthood next year."

"I believe I know the man," interrupted Lestrade. "Remember that bad business at Bisset's jewelry shop a few years back, Mr. Holmes? Two of our constables were badly wounded, and it was Dr. Saxonhouse who somehow managed to save both their lives. Do you know he slept in the same room at the hospital as the two constables for three nights until he was sure they would recover? I asked him if he didn't have a wife or family to go home to, and all he said was, 'Humanity is my family.'"

"He is the kindest, most thoughtful gentleman you could ever hope to meet," added the *maître d'*. "Although I will say I did see another side of him on one occasion."

Lestrade's interested was instantly piqued. "What side was that?"

"It was last year," answered the *maître d'*, "in the middle of summer, a dreadfully hot day, and I had stepped outside to get a breath of fresh air. The road was crowded with people and carriages, when one of the horses suddenly collapsed to the ground not twenty feet in front of me. No doubt it was overcome with the heat, and my heart went out to the poor creature as people gathered around to try and help. But the carter jumped down from his seat and began beating the poor beast unmercifully with a stick. It was horrible to witness, and my voice joined many others in beseeching the man to stop, but he was relentless as the horse began to scream in agony. It was then that I saw Dr. Saxonhouse forcing his way through the crowd, with a wild look in his eye that I remember to this day. He didn't say a word, but when he reached the carter he swung his walking stick at his head with such violence that the heartless villain collapsed to the ground senseless. When Dr. Saxonhouse turned and saw me, he came towards me, and in a voice trembling with emotion said, 'Get a veterinarian for that poor horse, but leave that swine where he lays.'"

As the *maître d'* gathered up some of our empty plates, a blanket of silence descended over us, and it was Lestrade who found his voice first. "If I could possibly have a small glass of port?" he enquired. I seconded this request, and was surprised when Holmes deigned to join us. The *maître d'* quickly made his way back into the kitchen, and only moments later we had three crystal glasses of ruby red port in our hands as we looked at one another.

"Good God," began Lestrade. "What now?"

"It would seem," I offered, searching for the right words, "that on the one hand Dr. Saxonhouse is almost a saint in human form, but on the other hand he doesn't respond well to witnessing innocent creatures or people being violently abused."

Holmes's gazed was fixed on the fluid in his glass. "And is that a crime?" he asked rhetorically. "Perhaps more importantly, has Dr. Saxonhouse spared Lord Chesterfield's new fiancée the grisly fate of his first wife?"

"Mr. Holmes," began Lestrade, "my sympathies are entirely with yours, but the fact of the matter is that there was a murder here, a murder that is our duty to solve."

"Quite right," agreed Holmes. "Let me see if I can solve it to the satisfaction of the local constabulary."

Holmes looked across the dining room, beckoned with his hand, and a moment later Constables Boswell and MacDuff were headed our way, like greyhounds who had just been released from the slips. Having observed our lack of conversation and activity, they had deduced that some conclusion had been reached and were anxious to be apprised of the news. Both men were bright-eyed and almost breathless as they arrived at our table and looked at Holmes.

"Have you done it, Mr. Holmes?" asked Boswell.

"You solved the murder?" added MacDuff.

"Well, of course he has!" enthused Boswell. "He's Sherlock Holmes!"

"Of course he has!" agreed MacDuff.

Holmes's sombre gaze drifted from me to Lestrade, but when he lifted his face to the two constables, somehow he had conjured up a pleasant smile.

"You are very kind, gentlemen," he began, "and I deeply appreciate your faith in my meagre abilities. Yes, I believe I have solved the murder, but I would impress upon you that it is only a theory. Would you care to hear it?"

Holmes may as well have asked a pair of terriers if they would like a rasher of bacon, as both constables were fairly jumping out of their skin with excitement. Slowly, Holmes extricated himself from the booth and pulled himself up to his full height.

"Quite a remarkable case," he began, "and one that I believe is unique in the annals of crime."

Holmes moved closer to the corpse of Lord Chesterfield, and as Constables MacDuff and Boswell practically danced around him, Lestrade and I both exited the booth and exchanged glances of apprehension.

Dedicated readers of these tales will recall that I have on occasion remarked upon Holmes's abilities as an actor, and it was now that he may as well have strolled onto the stage at the Lyceum Theatre to play the role for which he was born. Pointing to the scene of the crime, he began to lecture Boswell and Mac-Duff.

"I will keep this brief and to the point. Consider the scenario before us, gentlemen. The serving trolley has just arrived, the lids are lifted off the salvers, and our waiter Georgios drives the fork into the roast, then picks up the carving knife with the intention of cutting off pieces of the roast for our noble diner. However, our diner spies an item that causes him to fly into a paroxysm of rage; namely, the pot of horseradish that I found on the floor beneath the table. His fury is such that he wishes to strike out at the unfortunate waiter standing before him. The waiter is out of reach, and so our diner grabs the pot of horseradish with the intent of using it as a weapon. Being seated doesn't give him proper leverage, as he wishes to hurl the pot with maximum force, so he gets to his feet, using one hand to balance himself on the table. The other hand grasps the pot of horseradish, which is then thrown with sufficient force to cause a considerable contusion on the forehead of Georgios."

Holmes paused in his recitation to take in the reaction of Boswell and MacDuff, who I believe had both stopped breathing. Encouraged, Holmes continued with a flourish of his right arm that would have done Sir Henry Irving proud.

"Stunned by the blow, but still wishing to accommodate Lord Chesterfield's wishes, Georgios rushes for the kitchen and drops the carving knife down on this small shelf here at the back of the booth, not being mindful of the danger of the manner in which it is placed, with the point of the blade projecting towards the booth, and the end of the handle being jammed against this small lip of wood. Observe, gentlemen, these small drops of still moist grease from where the knife was laid."

Both Boswell and MacDuff instantly scrutinized the wooden shelf, before Boswell turned his face to Holmes in awe. "How did you find that, Mr. Holmes?"

"By looking for it, my dear Boswell. Shall I continue?"

Boswell and MacDuff nodded in unison as Holmes cleared his throat for his grand finale.

"The pot of horseradish, meanwhile, had rolled beneath the table, and when Lord Chesterfield attempted to adjust his position to hurl further abuse upon Georgios on his way to the kitchen, he inadvertently stepped on the pot of horseradish and lost his balance. Being somewhat elderly and not particularly athletic, he was unable to brace himself as he fell back heavily into the booth, thereby impaling himself on the blade of the knife through the weight and force of his own body. He then collapsed face first onto the table as we see him now, dying almost instantly due to a severed aorta. Providence, with a keen sense of poetic justice, had determined that the final victim of Lord Chesterfield's violent temper would be none other than himself. *Quod erat demonstrandum.*"

Constables Boswell and MacDuff stared at Holmes in something approaching rapture, and I believe would have broken out into applause had Inspector Lestrade not been standing right there. It was to Lestrade that Holmes now turned.

"Unless you happen to have a different theory, Lestrade?"

It was difficult to read the cascading thoughts and emotions clearly enveloping the Inspector, but after a moment he held out his hand. "By George, Mr. Holmes, you've done it again!"

As the two men shook hands, Boswell and MacDuff scampered off to inform their colleagues of the successful conclusion to the case. I looked at Holmes.

"With all due respect, Holmes," I began, "it's slightly terrifying that you can come up with something so ridiculous and so plausible at the same time."

"Indeed," agreed Lestrade.

"I could give you half-a-dozen other plausible explanations should you wish," replied Holmes. "The mark of any good investigator is an imagination that seeks out multiple solutions before choosing the best one."

As we made our way back to the lobby of the restaurant, Lestrade was clearly deep in thought, but kept nodding to himself as he dismissed one objection after another. Seeing us to the door, he shook both of our hands.

"I'll handle the rest of this affair along the lines suggested by Mr. Holmes. I can't say that my mind is entirely easy, but I know that London is a better place than it was earlier today, and that's good enough for me."

Moments later, as Holmes and I were in a carriage on our way back to Baker Street, I felt compelled to ask him a single question.

"Do you have any misgivings at all regarding this evening's events?"

"Just one," answered Holmes as he looked out the carriage window. "I fear that Dr. Saxonhouse may suffer a bout of conscience tomorrow and turn himself in to the police. I therefore propose to make any early morning call on him to explain how the matter stands, and to assure him that he can continue to provide the estimable services of his profession to Londoners of all stripes."

"And your conscience?" I asked.

"Perfectly clear," answered Holmes. "The horse being beaten in the street by Lord Chesterfield would have defended itself if it could. Similarly, Georgios would have defended himself against Lord Chesterfield's assault were he not a newly arrived immigrant in need of a job. Self-defence isn't a crime.

Nor, I would argue, is self-defence by proxy, which is the service that Dr. Saxonhouse exercised in both instances. Those of us who have the ability to act upon behalf of the downtrodden and persecuted have a sacred responsibility to do. That is the banner beneath which we march, Watson, and I'm very glad to have Dr. Saxonhouse in our ranks."

Holmes paused to gaze out the window at the passing images of London, still gleaming under a white blanket of newly fallen snow.

"It's a beautiful world, Watson. And the truth of the matter is that it becomes even more beautiful when some people leave it."

"Hear, hear," I nodded, and we rode the rest of the way back to our rooms in silence.

The Adventure of
Peter the Painter

Peter the Painter was a Latvian revolutionary who traveled to London and took part in the infamous Sidney Street Siege of 1911, after attempting to rob a jewelry store in Houndsditch. London policemen and then the Army itself did battle against two well-armed anarchists holed up at 100 Sidney Street. Peter was considered one of the most dangerous men in London and became famous as an anti-hero to the poverty-stricken denizens of London's East End. It is up to Holmes and Watson to track down this will-o'-the-wisp and bring him to justice; that is, if he ever existed in the first place.

If there is one truism that transcends all of human history, it's that a knock on the door at four in the morning never bodes well. So it was that in mid-December of 1910, I found myself being summoned from the arms of Morpheus by a distant rapping sound that was growing more frantic with every passing second. Emerging from my bedroom, I almost ran headlong into Holmes, who was in the process of putting on his dressing gown. As we locked eyes for a moment, there was no need for either of us to express our mutual understanding that we were about to learn of some kind of terrible event that could not wait until morning.

In theory, Holmes had retired to Sussex Downs some years ago, but research at the British Museum and various other affairs brought him up to London on a regular basis, where he always stayed with my wife and me in our cosy little abode in Queen Anne Street. Thankfully, my wife was off visiting her sister on this eventful morning, and moving down the stairs as rapidly as my still-stiff limbs would allow, I couldn't help but speculate upon who or what I might find upon opening the door.

A moment later I found myself gazing upon the pale complexion of Inspector Stanley Hopkins. Holmes made a habit of letting Scotland Yard know whenever he was in the city, and it was Hopkins who made the most use of Holmes's consultation services. In the present instance, he didn't say a word, but proceeded inside as I followed in his wake. Upon entering the sitting room, I saw that Holmes had already poured a snifter of brandy and was holding it out towards Hopkins, who reached for it eagerly.

"I suspect you need a drink, Inspector," said Holmes.

"Indeed I do." Hopkins took the glass and drained half of it in one gulp before sitting down and taking a long, shuddering breath. As I busied myself stoking the fireplace with fresh coal, Holmes took a seat opposite Hopkins and eyed him closely.

"It's a bad business," began Hopkins. "What on earth is the world coming to?"

"How many casualties?"

Hopkins looked up in surprise at Holmes's question, then nodded as he understood the logic behind it. "Of course. I wouldn't be here otherwise, would I? Five officers. There's been nothing like it. Not in the entire history of the Force."

Hopkins drained the rest of his glass and, as I moved to refill it, I could see him gathering himself to give Holmes as clear and concise a description of events as possible. For his part, in an effort to fully awaken himself and focus his mental faculties, Holmes stood up and gazed into the fire.

"Details," said Holmes curtly.

"There was an attempted robbery this evening at a jewelry store on Houndsditch," began Hopkins.

"The shop owned by Henry Harris?" enquired Holmes as I handed Hopkins more brandy.

"Precisely," answered Hopkins. "And this was no smash-and-grab operation, Mr. Holmes. Clearly, considerable time and planning went into it. The gang had apparently determined that Mr. Harris kept over £20,000 worth of jewels in the store's safe, and so they proceeded to rent No. 11 and No. 9 in the Exchange Buildings, which are only separated from the back of the jewelry store by a small yard. Just how long they have been planning this robbery we haven't yet determined, but we did recover a cylinder of compressed gas, a sixty-foot length of India rubber gas hose, and some diamond-tipped drills from the scene."

By now I had brought out my notebook and was rapidly scribbling down Hopkins's words as he took a sip of brandy and continued.

"We don't know how many people are in the gang, but last night they began to break through the back wall of the jewelry shop. They were overheard by one of the neighbors, who reported it to Constable Piper, who was walking his beat in the neighbourhood at the time. Piper also heard the noises, considered them suspicious, and walked around the block to knock on the front door of No. 11 in the Exchange Buildings."

"What made him choose that particular address?" asked Holmes.

"He noticed that it was the only property in the vicinity that had a light on in the back."

"Good man," answered Holmes. "Please go on."

"The door was opened, but only an inch or so, which immediately made Piper suspicious, and so he made an innocuous enquiry asking the man if his wife was in, and the man answered in a foreign accent that she was out. Piper said he would call back, then walked around to Houndsditch, where he saw a man acting suspiciously in the cul-de-sac. As Piper approached him, the man scuttled away into the shadows, and at this point Piper quite sensibly determined that he needed reinforcements. He was able to locate Constables Woodhams and Choate on their respective beats, then went to the Bishopsgate Station to report what was occurring. By 11:30, Piper returned to the scene with Sergeant Bentley and some other constables.

"Sergeant Bentley proceeded to knock on the door of No. 11 and asked the man who answered if anyone was doing work inside. The man didn't answer, but disappeared back into the building, prompting Bentley, Sergeant Bryant, and Constable Woodhams to follow him into the hall. Seeing another man standing on the stairs, Sergeant Bentley asked him to accompany them through to the back of the building.

"At that moment…" Hopkins faltered, then reached inside his coat for a small notebook. Opening it, he referred to his notes and continued in a halting voice.

"…at that moment another member of the gang opened the back door and began firing a gun. The man on the stairs began shooting as well. Sergeant Bentley was shot in the shoulder and neck. The second shot severed his spine. Constable Woodhams was shot in the upper leg and appears to have a shattered femur. Sergeant Bryant was shot in the arm and chest. The three men from the gang then attempted to escape, accompanied by a woman, but they encountered Sergeant Tucker in the cul-de-sac, who was shot through the heart and died instantly. Constable Choate managed to get hold of one of the gang, but his accomplices came to his assistance and Choate was shot twelve times. By this point the officers were able to return fire and wounded one of the gang, but he was carried away by his accomplices and they made their escape."

"I take it that the constables received firearms at the Station?" I asked.

Hopkins nodded, closed his notebook, and put it back inside his coat. "Constable Choate was taken to London Hospital and Sergeant Bentley is at Barts, but the doctors despair for both of their lives."

"And this gang," said Holmes, "I take it they were wholly unsuccessful insofar as their planned jewel heist was concerned?"

"They got nothing. The safe was unscathed."

"But who are they?" I asked. "Who would attempt such a bold and reckless crime?"

"Given the accent of the man who answered the door," returned Hopkins, "we suspect we're dealing with a group of criminals from Eastern Europe."

"Ah," I nodded. "That makes perfect sense."

"How so?" asked Holmes.

"A crime like that…well, let me just say that in my opinion it's entirely out of character for the typically phlegmatic British nature."

Holmes turned to look at Hopkins. "You say your men were able to wound one of the perpetrators?"

"Yes, sir. He cried out when he was hit and needed the help of his associates to flee the scene."

"It's unlikely they would take him to a hospital, so he may already be dead, or if the wound isn't that serious, the gang may have him hidden away until he can recover." Holmes paused to light his briar pipe. "Tell me something, Hopkins, do you have any officers who speak Russian or Yiddish?"

Judging by the inspector's expression, Holmes might just as well have asked him if he was hiding a polecat in his trousers. "Why no. Not to my knowledge. Do you happen to be familiar with either of those languages, Mr. Holmes?"

"I may possess a smattering," answered Holmes. "Enough to get by, at any rate. I'd like to examine the site, if I may, and speak to any witnesses."

"Thank you," said Hopkins. "I was hoping to get your opinion. But if you don't mind – "

"By all means visit your wounded comrades, Hopkins," said Holmes. "I would do the same in your position, and I know where the jewelry store on Houndsditch is."

"Shall I accompany you?" I asked.

"No need," answered Holmes as he pulled a revolver from a drawer. "I'm arming myself simply as a precaution. Whatever danger there was has likely passed and the perpetrators are now holed up somewhere licking their wounds. For the moment, I shall work better and more quickly on my own."

With that, Holmes and Hopkins left together, leaving me to jot down a few more notes, following which I did the only sensible thing I could think of, which was to go back to bed.

By the time I arose the following morning I expected Holmes to be back, but there was no sign of him, or any indication that he had returned while I was sleeping. Having my own duties to attend to, I busied myself with those, but as the noon hour passed I will confess to sneaking more than one glance up and down the street in the vain hope of seeing Holmes's tall, thin form striding rapidly along. It was only as three o'clock neared that I heard the front door open and the clatter of footsteps as Holmes shouted out instructions to the housekeeper.

"Hello! Food! Tea! Something! Thank you!"

A moment later the door was flung open and Holmes entered in a rush.

"Developments, Watson!" he began. "Things are proceeding apace! It is a nasty business to be sure."

Moving back to the door, he shouted down the stairs. "Sooner better than later! Thank you!"

As he turned back into the room, I brought out my notebook. "What's happened?"

He shook his head. "Regrettably, Constable Choate died early this morning. Sergeant Bentley was conscious when I spoke to him an hour ago, but when I talked privately with the doctors, they expressed doubt that he would last the day."

"Does he have family?"

"His quite evidently pregnant wife hasn't left his side for a moment."

"Good God." I was lost for words as Holmes went to the window and glanced up and down Queen Anne Street.

"Are you expecting visitors?" I asked.

"No, merely ascertaining that I wasn't followed back here. I took the usual precautions to conceal my tracks, but we are dealing with desperate people, and as of the moment we have no idea how large their organisation might be."

"What have you been able to determine so far?" I asked.

"After their escape from the scene, the gang made their way to Grove Street and holed up there. Concerned for their wounded accomplice, they summoned a doctor and explained away the bullet wound in his chest by saying that he had been accidently shot by an acquaintance. The wounded man's name was George Gardstein, and when the doctor recommended taking him to London Hospital, he refused to go. The doctor gave him some pain medication and said he would return shortly to check on his condition, but when the doctor came back, he found Gardstein dead on the bed. Having no knowledge of the events on Houndsditch, the doctor followed standard protocol and reported the death to the coroner. It took another hour before he passed along this information to the police. At that point, Hopkins and I made our way to Grove Street with several constables and found Gardstein's corpse on a bed. Where is that woman?"

"What woman?" I asked, genuinely confused.

Holmes made his way back to the door and as he flung it open, there stood my housekeeper with a tray. She gave a little cry of surprise as Holmes took the tray from her, "Thank you, my dear! You are a paragon among women!"

Closing the door with his foot, Holmes had already devoured half a sandwich before he put the tray down and poured himself a cup of tea.

"But that wasn't all that Hopkins and I found in Grove Street," he continued. "There was a woman there as well, a certain Sara Trassjonsky, who was busy burning as many papers as she could."

"Surely that isn't her real name," I interposed. "She would have made something up."

"Normally I would agree with you, of course," replied Holmes, "but the look in Hopkins's eye when he spoke to her wasn't something I have ever witnessed previously. I think she recognised it would be in her best interests to speak the truth, with the hope that our judicial system will be merciful to her on account of her gender."

"But why was she even there?" I asked. "Why hasn't she fled the city?"

"An excellent question," answered Holmes. "One would suspect some kind of allegiance or intimate association with Gardstein, but then, this is no mere gang of jewel thieves, Watson. We're dealing with Anarchists who have fled Russia for our more hospitable shores and who are determined to organise and launch their revolution from England. Of course, revolutions require capital and funding – hence their attempt to rob the jewelry store of Henry Harris."

"And what happened to this Sara Trassjonsky?"

"Arrested and currently enjoying accommodations at police headquarters in Old Jewry. I was able to have a short but productive private interview with her, with the understanding that I would communicate her cooperation to the police." Holmes paused to freshen his tea. "The papers she was attempting to burn were largely anarchist pamphlets and literature. Are you, perchance, familiar with any of their rhetoric or philosophy?"

"No," I returned. "I wouldn't poison my mind with such nonsense."

"Ah, then I suppose it's a good thing that I have never invited you along on any of my excursions to the Anarchist Club."

"Surely you're joking." I looked closely at Holmes, but his inscrutable expression gave nothing away. "You mean to tell me there is such a thing? An Anarchist Club in the heart of London?"

"It's in the East End. Jubilee Street, if you fancy a visit."

"Holmes, I don't understand. Why should you choose to associate yourself with that crowd? You're likely to get yourself assassinated!"

"It's always best to keep a finger on the pulse of every segment of society, whether you happen to sympathise with its ideology or not. As for the Anarchist Club, they aren't all wild-eyed bombers and revolutionaries. It's a social venue largely made up of Jewish émigrés from Russia."

"Still," I mused, "they fairly advertise their purpose with a name like the Anarchist Club. It's hard to believe the police haven't shut it down."

"Go to any meeting and it won't be long before you spot a plain-clothes policeman or two in attendance. They sincerely believe that their presence goes unnoticed, but they're as conspicuous as scorpions crawling over a tray of scones."

Holmes seemed inclined to continue, but something that had completely eluded me had evidently caught his attention.

"Do come in, Inspector Hopkins!" he announced. Sure enough, our door opened to reveal the haggard Hopkins, who shuffled his way slowly into the room.

"Help yourself to a sandwich and some tea, Inspector," said Holmes. "I was just filling Watson in on the case and its connection to the activities of the Anarchist Club."

"There is no question that last night's crime was hatched there," remarked Hopkins as he looked over the sandwiches. "But I've had two of my best undercover men in the club regularly and they had no clue that such an elaborate scheme was being planned."

"What have your men been able to learn, Inspector?" I asked.

"Very little," returned Hopkins. "They don't wish to make themselves known, and the language barrier is an issue as well. Regardless, they both feel certain they know who the mastermind behind the crime is – a gentleman known only as Peter the Painter."

"What makes your men suspect him?"

"Because he consciously makes himself conspicuous, which is no doubt intended to deflect attention from his activities behind the scenes." Hopkins was now pouring himself a cup of tea. "He's a tall, thin, dapper fellow, with a goatee and moustache that he waxes religiously."

"And he's a painter, you say?" I asked.

"No idea," answered Hopkins. "These people change professions and names from one day to the next. However, his bowler hat is marked with a splotch of red paint for some reason. Likely nothing more than an affectation to set him apart from the crowd."

"Or to identify him to Anarchists who may be new to London," I offered.

"Possibly. My men have attempted to follow him whenever he leaves the club, but without success. He is a will-o'-the-wisp who can apparently appear and disappear as he pleases. As you are no doubt aware, Doctor, the East End is a veritable warren of dark passageways and secret places. You could practically hide a herd of elephants there if you wished."

I turned to Holmes, who had listened attentively to Hopkins's recitation. "Then you should track him down! There isn't a man you couldn't trail if you wanted to, just as there isn't a man who could follow you if you didn't wish to be followed."

"You're very kind, Watson, but if this Peter the Painter was involved in last night's robbery, I suspect he will have gone to ground for the time being. Speaking of which, may I assume that this isn't merely a social visit, Hopkins? Is Mr. Gardstein ready for his session with the photographer?"

"As ready as he'll ever be, Mr. Holmes."

Holmes nodded and went upstairs to his bedroom. When he returned, carrying a small leather case, I asked, "What do you mean – session with a photographer? You said this Gardstein fellow was dead."

"Indeed I did. Your powers of recollection do you credit. Coming?"

Two minutes later Holmes, Hopkins, and I were out in the brisk air of Queen Anne Street. We strolled along in silence for several streets, but then it occurred to me that this was a propitious time to get a better understanding of these Anarchists and their goals. I posed this question to Holmes and, as expected, he rose to the occasion.

"If you study human history, Watson, you will find that in almost any oppressed community there exists a burning desire to become oppressors themselves. Where they were once persecuted, they now wish to persecute. Where they were miserable, they now seek to make the lives of others miserable. I recommend the example of the Pilgrims who left this country and settled in North America as an excellent illustration of this tendency. Similarly, these Russian expatriates, having fled the brutal caress of Mother Russia, now find themselves in an England that is relatively liberal by comparison. No longer under the thumb of the Czar and his secret police, some seek nothing more than better lives for themselves and their families, but others are almost exclusively focused on the destruction of society as we know it, particularly the upper class."

"Well," I answered, "while I would never sanction cold-blooded murder or the bombings of which these Anarchists are so fond, I will say that some of the excesses of the nobility and the wealthy do need to be reined in."

"Of course," returned Holmes. "And many of your fellow citizens heartily agree with you. But then, the Upper Ten Thousand, as they are termed, are extremely adept at manipulating social opinion through the press and by other means, so that the downtrodden and indigent are more often than not set at each other's throats, with the poor Englishman pitted against the poor foreigner rather than recognising and confronting their true oppressors and antagonists. Ah, but here we are."

Looking up, I saw that we had arrived at the stone steps leading up to The City of London Mortuary. With Hopkins leading the way, a few moments later we were gazing upon the quite deceased George Gardstein. With his mouth hanging open and streaks of blood on his face, he made for quite the grisly sight. Nearby, a photographer was in the process of setting up his camera as Holmes looked over the corpse disapprovingly.

"No, no, this won't do. Mr. Gardstein must be tidied up and made as presentable as we can make him." Holmes held up the case he had brought with him. "Luckily, we have just the tools for the job."

Opening the case, Holmes pulled out a sponge and a hairbrush and set to work as Hopkins and I looked on. I became aware that Holmes was actually humming to himself as he cleaned Gardstein up, something that Hopkins noticed as well. Just as the inspector was about to make some remark to me, Holmes stepped back from the corpse to display his handiwork.

"Well gentlemen, what do you think?"

The effect of Holmes's efforts, I must say, was truly remarkable. With his face clean, hair neatly coiffed, and eyes open, Gardstein appeared to have been resurrected.

"Excellent work, Mr. Holmes," said Hopkins. "If I didn't know better, I would say that Mr. Gardstein was still among the living."

"Then I should say he is quite ready for his appearance in tomorrow's newspapers." Holmes nodded to the photographer to get on with his work, then turned back to Hopkins. "What is the reward for any information on the whereabouts of Mr. Gardstein's associates?"

"One hundred pounds."

"No, no, no. That won't do. We need a figure large enough that news of it will spread quickly by word of mouth. Make it five hundred for whomever identifies the Houndsditch murderers and their current location."

"Of course." With a glance at the photographer, Hopkins took Holmes by the elbow. "If I might have a word."

As we emerged into the hallway, Hopkins glanced left and right and, having determined that we were alone, he leaned towards Holmes in conspiratorial fashion.

"While I feel quite sure that Gardstein's picture in the paper and the reward money will soon flush the rats out, there is something with which I could use your help."

"Do tell."

"It's regarding this Peter the Painter fellow. I have it on good account that in the past six months, he has planned any number of heists and even an assassination or two."

"But how is that possible?" I objected. "There hasn't been anything reported in the newspapers."

"Because there has been nothing to report," answered Hopkins. "What this Peter the Painter has failed to realise, at least so far, is that there is a traitor in his organisation who keeps us apprised of the various crimes these Anarchists intend to commit."

"Then what happened yesterday at the jewelry store on Houndsditch?" I asked.

"You have me there, Dr. Watson. We had no advance warning whatsoever."

"I believe I have an explanation," interposed Holmes, "should you wish to hear it."

"Of course." Hopkins looked at Holmes with the keen eyes of a terrier who has just heard the scurrying sound of a rat across a kitchen floor.

"In looking further into the matter, I was able to ascertain that all of the perpetrators of last night's crime are recently arrived from the region of Latvia, which is on the Baltic Sea in the northwestern corner of the Russian Empire. They appear to have kept their plan to themselves and didn't share it with the larger Anarchist community – which would include Peter the Painter."

"Did you learn that from the Trassjonsky woman?" asked Hopkins. "I couldn't get a word out of her."

"English is not her strong suit, Hopkins," answered Holmes. "Fortunately, I have a passing understanding of Russian, which seemed to set her at ease to a certain extent."

"What else did she tell you?"

"That Gardstein was the leader of the gang, although she may be saying that simply because he's dead and beyond the reach of justice. She lived with him in Warsaw six years ago, until they had to flee the city when he was accused of terrorism. They then combined forces with three other revolutionaries: Yakov Peters, Yourka Dubof, and Fritz Svaars, who is a cousin of Yakov Peters. Svaars had taken part in the 1905 Russian Revolution, but then fled the country when the insurrection failed. Between them, the three men then blazed a trail of murder and robberies across Europe until finally arriving in London. It was here that they met another Russian expatriate, William Sokoloff, who had been in London for about ten years and worked as a watchmaker and jeweler, but made a habit of stealing from his employers."

"And all this to what end?" I asked.

"To finance the overthrow of the Russian government – particularly Czar Nicholas and his family, for whom they all share a pathological hatred."

"Why? What did the Czar ever do to them?"

"As Russian Jews, they were all subject to the most appalling depredations imaginable. When Yakov Peters was jailed for handing out revolutionary pamphlets, all of his fingernails were torn out. Yourka Dubof was publicly flogged by the Czar's Cossacks until he lost consciousness. As for Miss Trassjonsky herself, she too suffered the unwelcome attentions of the Cossacks, although she refused to say anything more than that."

"It's a sorry tale, Mr. Holmes," remarked Hopkins, "but I'm afraid it doesn't give them license to come to England to prey upon people who have never lifted a finger against them."

"On the contrary, they see all of Europe's nobility as little more than an organised criminal family who are all related to one another and a cancer to be excised as quickly and bloodily as possible. Don't forget, Hopkins, our late sovereign, King Edward VII, was uncle to both Czar Nicholas II and Emperor Wilhelm II of Germany, and George V is a first cousin to both of them."

"Well, that's true enough," conceded Hopkins, "but my allegiance is to England, and more specifically to my fellow officers in Scotland Yard. I won't rest until every one of the men involved in last night's attempted robbery is standing on the gallows."

"Well then, get Gardstein's picture in the paper, along with the reward money being offered, and I suspect you won't have to wait long for news of their whereabouts."

"Very good, Mr. Holmes. I'll be sure to keep you posted on any developments."

"Please do," answered Holmes. "I'm as anxious to get these murderers off the streets as you are."

"And in regards to Peter the Painter," continued Hopkins, "I'm not going to pretend that I understand or condone all of your methods, but in this case, if you could possibly use your powers to track this fellow down, I would be most grateful. Whatever it takes. And you have my personal assurance that no questions will be asked."

The next morning's papers featured not only the lurid details of the Houndsditch murders, but also the photograph of the late George Gardstein and the sizable reward being offered for more information on the men who had murdered three policemen. Holmes glanced only briefly at the papers, then paced about the room like a nervous cat. One moment he was at the window, then he was attempting to read, then back at the window. Finally, I was startled by the sound of his fist slamming against the table.

"I am not well suited to this, Watson."

"To what?"

"Waiting. Passivity. Held to a complete standstill while waiting for someone else to do something. My entire being rebels against it."

"Perfectly understandable, but you can't very well conduct a house-to-house search of every building in London for these Anarchists."

"And I shouldn't have to. I should be able to put myself in the position of the perpetrators and logically narrow the parameters. But London is no longer the city it was when we first met. New streets and neighborhoods seemingly spring up overnight. In the past thirty years, the population has swollen by nearly three million people. I fear we may have reached a tipping point where informants and investigations will no longer be enough to hold the criminal elements at bay."

"You're saying that the Anarchists may very well win the day."

"If a sufficient percentage of any population feel aggrieved and that they have nothing to lose, then the society may very well fall into chaos, yes."

"Then maybe Hopkins is right," I began. "The solution lies with Peter the Painter. If you can locate him, surely the other pieces of the puzzle will fall into place. Perhaps he has borrowed a page from Poe's 'The Purloined Letter' and you'll find him at the Anarchist Club, hiding in plain sight."

"Unlikely," replied Holmes. "You can be certain that every entrance and exit to the Anarchist Club is now under surveillance by Hopkins and his men. We won't find our quarry there."

"Then what can we do?"

"As much as it pains me to say it, we wait. Time, like water, is an irresistible force. I feel certain there will be no more Anarchist crimes in the immediate future as they lick their wounds and wait for the hysteria surrounding the Houndsditch murders to abate. Bear in mind that not only will the police be looking for the murderers, so will the public, with their appetite whetted for the chase by the reward money being offered. All the same, however, I think I'll venture out, to ease my nerves if nothing else. You stay here and hold down the fort, as our American friends like to say. I expect events to start unfolding very quickly."

As much as I chafed at the thought of remaining at home as Holmes went out to pace the streets of London, I was also aware that I would struggle to keep up with him and that there wasn't much that we could do in terms of uncovering new information through investigating. Rather, as Holmes noted, that new information would come to us, courtesy of acquaintances, landlords, or observant citizens anxious to lay claim to the reward money.

Sure enough, the very next day, the police trumpeted the arrest of Osip Federoff, an unemployed locksmith who was a known Anarchist and associate of Gardstein, although there was no evidence linking him to the Houndsditch murders. There then followed three days with no further progress, and a memorial service for officers Tucker, Bentley, and Choate was planned for December 22nd at St. Paul's Cathedral. Hundreds of thousands of Londoners turned out to line the route to the cemeteries, with the London Stock Exchange closing down for half-an-hour to permit the brokers to watch the procession as it made its way down Threadneedle Street. That same day there appeared to be a major break in the case, as Yourka Dubof and Yakov Peters were both apprehended. However, when Federoff, Dubof, and Peters were charged with the murders of the three policemen at the Guildhall Police Court, they all pled not guilty. Of the notorious Peter the Painter there was no sign at all, and the press speculation was that he had fled the city and had already made his way to the Continent.

Increasingly, it appeared as if the two prime suspects in the Houndsditch murders were Fritz Svaars and William Sokoloff, but New Year's Eve came and went with no sign of them. Then a grisly discovery connected with the crime was found on Clapham Common in South London on New Year's Day. A Russian Jewish immigrant by the name of Léon Beron was discovered by a passerby severely beaten and semi-conscious, but what sent the press into a frenzy of speculation was that the letter "*S*" had been carved by a knife into both of his cheeks. Surely, this could be nothing less than a warning from Svaars and Sokoloff to any other Russian immigrants to keep their mouths shut. That meant they were still in London, and new hope arose that they would both be apprehended quite soon.

Holmes was out more than he was in, but whenever our paths crossed and I ventured a question, I was met with a non-committal shrug or merely a grunt of an answer. I could tell that the entire affair was weighing on him heavily and there was even some speculation that members of the Russian Secret Police (also known as the *Okhrana*) had arrived in London to deal with the Anarchists in their own fashion. Of course, the newspapers were having a field day with each new lurid detail that came to light, fanning the flames of prejudice against practically every immigrant in the East End, proposing one outlandish theory after another regarding the whereabouts of Svaars and Sokoloff, and what crimes they might be planning next. For his part, Peter the Painter was built up to be a criminal mastermind of Professor Moriarty's proportions.

Just as I was thinking of going to bed on the evening of January 2nd, a rather frantic pounding on the front door sent me scurrying down the stairs to find a breathless Hopkins standing on the front step.

"Hopkins!" I exclaimed. "I'm afraid – "

"I know Mr. Holmes isn't here!" Hopkins cut me off. "But he's done it! We know where they are! Get your coat if you want to be there when we put the cuffs on them. Just be sure to put in a good word for Scotland Yard if you decide to write this up as one of your stories."

Scarcely a minute later, Hopkins and I were rattling along at high speed in a police automobile. Anticipating every question on my lips, Hopkins filled me in.

"I told Mr. Holmes I wouldn't ask any questions regarding his methods and I won't, but late yesterday he sent a note to Scotland Yard saying that Sokoloff and Svaars were holed up at 100 Sidney Street, and requesting £500 in cash for his informant. We've had the address under surveillance all day, and there was a meeting with the City Police and the Metropolitan Police this afternoon to decide what to do."

"Why not just enter the building in force and arrest them?" I asked.

"If only it were that simple, Doctor. We feel certain that these men are very well-armed, and there are dozens of tenants in the building. We can't run the risk of any innocent people being taken as hostages, so we need to evacuate everyone without rousing the suspicions of Svaars and Sokoloff. We just started that process an hour or two ago to accomplish it under the cover of the night."

"And what of Holmes?" I asked.

"I'm sure he's in the vicinity," returned Hopkins, "and I trust him to be able to take care of himself. The same goes for you, because anything might happen when we try to arrest those men. It could go wrong very quickly."

In all candour, I will confess that I was utterly unprepared for the sight that awaited me as we arrived in Sidney Street. I was expecting a handful of policemen and vehicles, but as I glanced around in wonder at the cordoned off area outside 100 Sidney Street, I estimated there to be no fewer than two hundred officers in the area. The building itself was three stories high, and many of the people who had been evacuated from it remained on hand to watch the proceedings. Some of them had apparently summoned friends and relatives for what they anticipated would be a memorable event. Holmes was nowhere to be seen, and Svaars and Sokoloff, the only two people left in the building, seemed to be quite unaware of what was transpiring outside. Spotting Hopkins in a heated conversation with what I took to be some governmental official, I waited until the gentleman had stalked off in high dudgeon before I approached the inspector.

"He wants us to storm the building right now, but I'm not having it," seethed Hopkins. "Those men are on the top floor, and the only way up there is a winding stairwell in which two men can barely stand abreast. I'm not about to bury any more officers if I can help it. There's nothing for it but to wait until dawn so we can see what we're doing."

"Perhaps the two of them will surrender once they see what they're up against," I offered optimistically.

Hopkins turned his face away from me and I could see him attempting to master the emotions that threatened to overwhelm him. "Look around you, Dr. Watson. All of these officers just lost colleagues who were murdered in cold blood. And the two men in that building know very well that if they make it out alive, the only future they have will be at the end of a rope. This is the calm before the storm, and we can only hope that the storm passes quickly."

At that, Hopkins strode off to consult further with his men, and I became uncomfortably aware of the fact that despite the hour, the number of curious bystanders was steadily growing. By the time the first tendrils of dawn crept over the horizon, there was the general feeling that at any moment, something momentous was about to take place. At some signal that I didn't see, a single policeman approached the front door of the building and knocked loudly. The gathered crowd held its collective breath as the officer knocked at the door again, but with no response. He was then joined by another constable, and together they gathered up some stones and began flinging them high into the air and against the windows on the top floor.

It was at that moment, just as I turned to see how the crowd was reacting to this new development, that I saw a distinctive figure that had been thoroughly described to me only days earlier. He was about fifty yards from where I stood – tall, thin, with a goatee and upturned moustache, a high white collar, and a red blotch of paint on the side of his black bowler hat. It was none other than Peter the Painter. It had to be.

As I began to move towards him, there was a collective gasp from the crowd, and as I looked up at 100 Sidney Street I saw the figures of two men who had been roused from their slumber at one of the windows. Before the police could say or do anything, the two men smashed out the window and began firing down below. An instant later I saw a police sergeant fall to the ground clutching his chest, and as his colleagues ran to his aid a swell of movement in the crowd practically lifted me off my feet, and I soon found myself thirty yards from my original location through no volition of my own.

The crowd scattered for cover as the police returned fire, and as the chaos grew I lost sight of Peter the Painter, who was swallowed up in the sea of humanity. Some were fleeing for their lives, but others were more intent on jostling for a better view, and as the waves of bodies crashed against one another, I felt the very breath being crushed out of me. In my naivete, I had fully expected the whole incident to be over once the shooting began and the police returned fire, but that proved to be far from the case. As the minutes passed, it was clear that Svaars and Sokoloff had superior weapons to the police, as well as an abundance of ammunition at their disposal. Hopkins and the other authorities present were disinclined to send any of their men on a suicide mission into the building, and from my protected vantage point I was able to see them huddled together in frantic consultation at what they should do next.

By ten o'clock, the answer came as a detachment of Scots Guards appeared on the scene and began taking up positions in the buildings across the street from the Anarchists and at both ends of the street. I would learn later that they had been summoned from The Tower of London where they were stationed, and that it was the first time the military had joined forces with the police to end an armed siege in London. However, even these reinforcements failed to turn the tide in favor of the authorities as more and more curious citizens flocked to the area. By noon, there was at least one Pathé News camera filming the events, and Home Secretary Winston Churchill had arrived on the scene as well, much to the displeasure of the crowd, who blamed the Liberal Party's immigration policies for allowing these Anarchists to come to England in the first place.

It was just short of one o'clock in the afternoon when smoke began to emerge from the second story windows of the building, and when a representative of the London Fire Brigade requested permission to attempt to extinguish the blaze, he was promptly turned down by the police, who by this point were quite happy to watch the building burn with the two men still inside. The shooting coming from Svaars and Sokoloff soon ceased, and when part of the roof collapsed, the Fire Brigade was given permission to stop the blaze from spreading to nearby buildings. It took a few more hours, but eventually the charred corpses of Svaars and Sokoloff were pulled from the ruined building, the crowd dispersed, and I began to make my way back home, still having never caught a single glimpse of Holmes. To my surprise, as I trudged along, still trying to make sense of the events of the day, Inspector Hopkins came by in a police vehicle and offered me a lift back to Queen Anne Street.

Shaken by all of the events that we had just witnessed, we rode in silence, and when I disembarked, Hopkins did the same and we made our way inside. It was with some relief that we found Holmes in residence, smoking his cherry-wood pipe and staring into a well-stoked fire. He turned as Hopkins and I entered and remarked, "A sorry day in the history of London. I have already taken the liberty of helping myself to a brandy, and I heartily recommend that you do the same, gentlemen."

Hopkins and I lost no time in pouring two snifters, and after his first sip Hopkins observed, "A sorry day indeed, but a necessary one. I can only hope that the Anarchists learn from this and realise that they cannot escape English justice if they choose to bring their fight to these shores."

"They will take their revolution back to Russia soon enough," said Holmes. "Their failed uprising in 1905 served largely as a training exercise. If he had any wits at all, the Czar would realise this, but sadly, the nobility aren't noted for their sagacity."

"I do want to thank you, Mr. Holmes," continued Hopkins, "for all of your help. But if I may be so bold, may I ask you a question? Just between us?"

"Yes?" Holmes eyed Hopkins keenly.

"There is only one of the Anarchists that we failed to apprehend or bring to justice – Peter the Painter. Forgive me for saying so, but it leads me to believe that he was the source of your information on the whereabouts of Svaars and Sokoloff. Perhaps in exchange for that, you aided him in his disappearance?"

"No."

"I have your word on that?"

"Peter the Painter doesn't exist."

To say that Hopkins and I were both shocked beyond measure at Holmes's calm pronouncement doesn't do justice to the incredulous look that we exchanged before we turned back to Holmes.

"But he does!" I fairly shouted. "I saw him!"

"Saw him?" Holmes raised an eyebrow. "Saw him where?"

"In Sidney Street as dawn was breaking. He was just as Hopkins described him. Tall, thin, with a goatee, and an upturned moustache. And he had a splotch of red paint on his hat!"

"Are you sure that's what you saw, Watson? In the dim light of the morning? After being up all night? Would you be willing to swear to that in court? Or did you only see what your mind had prepared you to see?"

"I…" Hesitating, I tried to conjure up the precise image that I had observed for a few fleeting moments before utter chaos ensued. "I could have sworn – "

"Well, then," chimed in Hopkins as I faltered, "if Peter the Painter doesn't exist, how would you explain this?"

Reaching into his coat, Hopkins removed what was quite clearly a bowler hat that had seen much better days. It was battered, muddy, and flattened, with an unmistakable blotch of red paint on it. Hopkins handed the hat to Holmes, who proceeded to push and prod it into something vaguely resembling its original shape. Holding the hat at arm's length, Holmes looked at it and pronounced, "It would appear to be a bowler hat with a splotch of red paint on it. Recently recovered from Sidney Street, I take it?"

Hopkins nodded, "And I think we may assume it was trampled in the stampede that followed the first shots ringing out."

"Not an injudicious assumption," agreed Holmes as he put the hat down.

"Mr. Holmes, I will simply thank you again for your services in this case with no further uncomfortable questions. Quite frankly, I don't particularly care whether you paid this Peter the Painter off or are seeking to give him time to flee the country, but I must insist upon your assurance on one point."

"Name it."

"That I will never see nor hear of Peter the Painter in London again."

"You have my word, Hopkins."

"Excellent. Then with that let us put this entire sorry affair behind us." Hopkins turned to me, inclined his head slightly, and then he was gone, leaving me to gape at Holmes in some wonderment.

"So let me understand," I began, "you were in consultation with this Peter the Painter all along?"

"Watson, I suggest that we take Hopkins's most excellent advice and put this case behind us."

"But why? What kind of power – what hold does this Peter the Painter have over you?"

"He's gone, Watson," returned Holmes. "If that's enough for Hopkins, it should be enough for us."

"But you could find him from his hat alone!" I insisted as I picked up the battered bowler. "Do you remember the case of the Blue Carbuncle, and the astonishing deductions you were able to make regarding Mr. Henry Baker simply from examining his hat? You were able to describe his wife, his home, the decline in his fortunes. Here – " I thrust the hat at Holmes and he took it. "Take one minute to examine this closely and I feel certain that it will shed light on the whereabouts of Peter the Painter."

"Very well." Holmes picked up his lens and proceeded to subject the hat to a close inspection. "The gentleman in question would appear to be middle-aged, but in good physical condition. Given to bursts of energy, he is also capable of barely moving for days at a time – both a consequence of his somewhat unique profession, which necessitates the work coming to him, rather than him pursuing the work. Semi-retired and unmarried, he currently lives in the southeast of England, but makes regular trips to London, where he stays with a friend of his. This friend is a professional man, most likely a doctor with a literary bent, and an occasional pawky sense of humour."

And as Holmes cast a glance at me out of the corner of his eye, he placed the hat on his own head. "Found him."

In the course of my association with Sherlock Holmes, I have experienced any number of bizarre and strange situations, but as those two simple words left Holmes's lips, I was so stunned that it felt as if reality itself was dissolving in front of my very eyes.

"You?" I finally managed. "You mean to say that *you're* Peter the Painter? But why?"

Removing the bowler from his head, Holmes turned it in his hands thoughtfully. "When I became aware of the number of Anarchists flooding into London, I realised it was only a matter of time before they embarked on a campaign of assassinations and bombings to bring attention to their cause, as they had elsewhere in Europe. Given that, the choice was between reacting to events after they happened, or to somehow be able to anticipate and forestall events before they occurred. I couldn't very well go to the Anarchist Club as Sherlock Holmes, and so I simply invented a new identity for myself – that of Peter the Painter. As you are aware, my grandmother was the sister of Horace Vernet, the French artist, and so it seemed to be a suitable role for me to play. Through the judicious use of spirit gum, I was able to apply a beard and moustache, a light application of make-up was enough to take a few years off my appearance, and a high collar completed the effect by obscuring the skin on my neck, which is always the surest way to mark an individual's age.

"Presenting myself as a first-generation Englishman with Russian parents, I was able to quickly establish my utility to their cause thanks to my familiarity with London, excellent English, and passable Russian. I was also able to take the heated rhetoric I heard inside the walls of the Anarchist Club and suggest utterly plausible schemes that somehow always ended up being thwarted at the last moment, as I anonymously passed the necessary information on to the police. The important thing was to make the Anarchists feel that they were taking action, even if this robbery or that assassination never quite succeeded. Sadly, in the case of Mr. Gardstein and his associates, they were all Latvian and distrusted anyone not in their immediate circle. They were able to plan their robbery of the jewelry store on Houndsditch with no one in the Anarchist Club having any inkling of what they were up to – not even Peter the Painter, who would, of course, have informed the police had he known."

"And I take it that it was in the guise of Peter the Painter that you found the informant who revealed the whereabouts of Svaars and Sokoloff."

"Correct. He wanted the reward money, but was afraid of going to the police directly."

"Then why on earth were you in Sidney Street earlier today as Peter the Painter?"

"Ah. There we enter the dark and troubling world of authority figures trying to exercise their authority just to prove that they have it. It was the Metropolitan Police who coordinated the evacuation of the building, but during the long night vigil, as we waited for dawn to break, the higher-ups among the City Police became convinced that Svaars and Sokoloff had somehow slipped out when the other tenants were being evacuated and were no longer in the building. As you can imagine, the discussion on this point between representatives of the two police forces was extremely spirited and threatened to undermine the entire operation. Fortunately, I was able to notify my informant, and for an additional one-hundred pounds, he was able to verify that Svaars and Sokoloff were still there this morning – but he insisted upon receiving his payment in person from Peter the Painter himself."

"Very well then," I observed, "Hopkins may be satisfied, but what about the press? What about the government? I saw Home Secretary Churchill on Sidney Street watching it all unfold. There will be questions and an investigation, with at least part of it surrounding the identity and whereabouts of Peter the Painter."

"They are entitled to investigate and ask as many questions as they wish, but in this case, I'm afraid I will have no answers." Holmes stepped nearer the fire and tossed the bowler into the flames. "When the accounts of the events on Houndsditch and Sidney Street are written, Peter the Painter will remain nothing more than an enigma. After all, Watson, what's life without a little mystery?"

With that, Holmes went upstairs to his bedroom and closed the door behind him, leaving me to gaze into the fire, where the only evidence of Peter the Painter's existence was burning itself into ashes. Sure enough, in the coming weeks and months there were many things written about what came to be known as the Siege of Sidney Street, and there was considerable speculation regarding the mysterious figure of Peter the Painter. Had he fled to the Continent? Had he been murdered by his fellow Anarchists? Various very clever people proposed various very clever answers, but not one account came near to the truth of the matter – that the mysterious Peter the Painter had never existed at all.

NOTE

The events surrounding the Siege of Sidney Street (aka The Battle of Stepney) are much as described in the above story. In January 1911, London police found themselves in a pitched battle against heavily-armed Latvian anarchists, who had murdered three policemen the previous month. Winston Churchill himself came to personally view the unfolding drama, and the mysterious figure of Peter the Painter figured prominently in newspaper accounts of the time, but his real name was never discovered and he subsequently disappeared, never to be seen or heard of again.

The Amateur Mendicant Society

Alluded to by Dr. Watson in "The Five Orange Pips," this un-chronicled case of Sherlock Holmes from 1887 has intrigued fans of the great detective for decades. What could possibly distinguish a group of amateur beggars and make it worthy of the attention of Sherlock Holmes? Perhaps if the name of the society is as misleading as the people who are members, and perhaps if one of those members has homicide on his mind.

Readers who have been kind enough to cast an occasional eye over these short tales related to the activities of my friend, Sherlock Holmes, may recall that in "The Five Orange Pips," I made passing reference to a few of the cases that had come to his attention in 1887. Among them were the adventure of the Paradol Chamber, the sinking of the British barque *Sophy Anderson*, and the bizarre series of events concerning the Grice Patersons on the island of Uffa. Some of Holmes's more ardent admirers have upbraided me over the years by noting that there is no "island of Uffa" in existence, which is quite correct. Indeed, I have an entire file brimming with letters from various cranks who seem to take special pride in attempting to correct my supposed errors and mistakes, apparently unaware that I regularly used alternative names for places and people in an effort to shield the privacy of individuals whose only crime was to be the victim of a crime.

With the passage of time, I feel more comfortable in revealing that "Uffa" was my pseudonym for the Isle of Arran, which can be found in the Firth of Clyde on Scotland's west coast. With that mystery solved, let me address the unwritten case which, aside from "The Giant Rat of Sumatra," has caused the most comment among the followers of Mr. Sherlock Holmes – namely, "The Adventure of the Amateur Mendicant Society."

This too occurred in 1887, and part of my reluctance in telling this tale is due to the fact that Holmes and I were both present when the crime occurred, and to this day it remains one of the most horrific scenes I have ever witnessed in my life.

If I cast my mind back to the early months of 1887, I recall thinking that it was destined to be one of the most cursed years in the annals of British history. In January, the British ship *Kapunda* had collided with the barque *Ada Melmoure* off the coast of Brazil and had sunk so rapidly that no lifeboats could be launched, with over three hundred poor souls perishing in the waters of the Atlantic. In February, an underground explosion had killed thirty coal miners in Wales, and in March, *The Times* had disgraced itself by publishing a series of letters intended to ruin the reputation of Charles Stewart Parnell, with the letters subsequently proven to be outright forgeries.

Then, as the sun progressively rose in the sky to announce the coming of spring, I was pleased that the news, like the weather, became better and better. In May, I had greatly enjoyed the opening of Buffalo Bill's Wild West Show, where I was positively astonished at the displays of bronco riding, calf roping, and the appearance of several members of the Ogala Lakota tribe, not to mention the magnetic personality of William Cody himself. This exhibition, it will be recalled, was part of the Golden Jubilee of Queen Victoria, and a command performance was given for the Queen herself in June. That same month, Holmes was discreetly consulted regarding what came to be known as the Jubilee Plot, which was ostensibly a plan by radical Irish nationalists to assassinate the Queen and blow up Westminster Abbey. However, as Holmes quickly determined, it was a rather disgraceful attempt by the British government itself to stir the Fenians up in an effort to justify further violence against them. Aside from this and a few other minor blemishes, all of the Golden Jubilee ceremonies and activities proved to be an unqualified triumph for Her Majesty.

And so, time trundled on, as it is wont to do, and before I knew it the days had shortened, the temperature had fallen, and upon glancing at the calendar on this particular morning, I had been mildly discomfited to discover that Christmas Day was almost upon us. When I had ventured out for a morning newspaper, I found Baker Street more crowded than usual, with countless carriages and pedestrians scurrying to-and-fro on what I suspected were various shopping expeditions and other excursions related to the upcoming holiday.

Now settled in front of the fire with my paper, I was dimly aware that Holmes's tall, lean figure had been staring out into the slanting morning light for some time, when a sharp intake of his breath made me look up. He turned, nodding to himself, then looked at me.

"Why not?"

"Excellent question, Holmes," I responded. "Why not, indeed?"

Holmes offered a thin smile by way of answer. "As much as I appreciate your agreeable nature, Watson, you haven't the faintest idea to what I am referring."

"On the contrary," I returned. "It's obviously a question of whether you take the case or not. Don't imagine you're the only person in these rooms capable of the occasional deductive insight."

"Interesting." Holmes took the seat across from me and fixed me with a steady stare. "If you would care to explain your reasoning process, I would be most grateful. How did the two words '*Why not*' reveal to you the innermost workings of my mind?"

"It's quite elementary," I began, working mightily to keep the smile off my face. "Those words coming from almost anyone else would convey a universe of possibilities: *Why not go for a walk? Why not make the acquaintance of a particular individual? Why not purchase a periodical or have roast mutton for dinner?* With Sherlock Holmes, however, his interests are

88

confined to a much narrower spectrum than most other people – specifically: *Cases*. To take them or not to take them. That is the entirety of his universe. So then, quite a commonplace deduction."

I returned my attention to my newspaper and was gratified to hear a small laugh coming from Holmes. "Well, well, well. Clearly, I sit before you with every nook and cranny of my private thoughts on full display. It would be useless to deny it, so would you care to accompany me to the Bank of England for a private conference with two gentlemen regarding the Amateur Mendicant Society?"

"The what?" I answered, setting down my paper.

"Oh dear," said Holmes. "You don't say that the Amateur Mendicant Society has somehow eluded the net of your omniscience? Get your coat and I shall endeavour to explain as we make our way to the City."

It was only a few minutes later that Holmes and I found ourselves rattling along in a hansom cab in the direction of Threadneedle Street. Holmes gazed around at the kaleidoscope of passing London as he spoke.

"The fact of the matter is," he began, "very few people have any awareness of the Amateur Mendicant Society. I hasten to add that this isn't due to any nefarious activities on their part. London is positively awash in various clubs and societies, largely because of men looking for any excuse to escape the watchful eyes of their wives and mothers. If a man has access to this or that club and frequents it on a regular basis, it serves as an excellent excuse to avoid the more unpleasant areas of a domesticated life."

"Come now," I chided. "There are many men who look forward to time with their wives and children and quiet evenings at home."

Was that an involuntary shudder I saw pass through Holmes? "If you say so," he answered. "But now to the activities of the Amateur Mendicant Society. What do you suppose they do with themselves? Why does the society exist?"

"Well, they're beggars of some type, yes? That's what a mendicant is – a kind of religious beggar, I believe."

"In theory," returned Holmes, "but would you expect to have a conference with two religious beggars at the Bank of England?"

"I suppose not."

"Precisely. No, Watson, their name is an attempt at somewhat ironic humour. These particular mendicants are all very well-to-do. Some of it is inherited money, some of it is due to industrious enterprise, and some of it is due to successfully navigating their way to the public trough through various bribes and connections. Nevertheless, the putative goal of these mendicants is to solicit money from the public, but to keep none of it for themselves. Rather, it is then distributed to the more unfortunate members of the community. They are a charitable organisation *ne plus ultra.*"

"Excellent!" I enthused. "It's always gratifying to hear of people trying to make the world a better place. Why have they contacted you?"

"I'm not entirely clear on that," answered Holmes. "Their missive was brief and to the point, but apparently a shadow of some concern has recently fallen across the Society. We are meeting the two chief officers of the Society at the Bank of England because that is where they are both employed. But here, all of our questions will soon be answered."

As we turned a corner, the Bank came into full view in all its splendour. The remarkable design of architect John Soane had created a veritable island of solid stone to convey the absolute permanence and trustworthiness of this venerable institution, and moments later Holmes and I were striding between two massive pillars into the interior of the building. Upon communicating the nature of our visit, we were swiftly conducted to the office of the Deputy Governor. He rose from his desk at our entrance and strode towards us with a smile on his face and his hand outstretched.

"Mr. Holmes and Dr. Watson," he began. "This is, indeed, a pleasure. I am Trevor Granville."

As we shook hands, I took stock of Mr. Granville and his office. Both were large and inviting, and I feared for the links in the gold watch chain that was stretched taut across his considerable bulk. His warm brown eyes glistened with friendliness as he directed Holmes and me to chairs near his desk. Bookshelves crowded with leather-bound volumes lined the walls, and perched upon various pedestals and shelves were what I took to be either replicas or originals of ancient Greek pottery. On the wall behind his desk was a rather remarkable oil painting of a man wearing a crown and surrounded by gold coins, facing a rather pained-looking gentleman being held by what I took to be two courtiers.

"My colleague, Mr. Hurst, will join us shortly," said Granville as he settled himself into a well-padded armchair.

As was his custom, Holmes's eyes had scanned the room, taking in every detail, before finally landing on the painting. "King Croesus, I presume?"

"Yes, indeed!" Granville nodded enthusiastically. "The old boy being put in his place by Solon the Athenian. Are you familiar with the story?"

"I'm afraid not," I answered.

"Well, Croesus, as you know," began Granville, "is generally regarded as the wealthiest man who ever lived. When he granted an audience to Solon the Athenian, he was most anxious to ask him who was the happiest man in the world, fully expecting that Solon would say King Croesus himself, due to his inestimable riches. However, Solon proceeded to confound Croesus' expectations by listing men who had led selfless and exemplary lives dedicated to helping other people, which infuriated Croesus. It's my little reminder to myself that money isn't everything – although in all candor, it is most things. Ah, but here is Mr. Hurst!"

True enough, a slim, mournful-looking man had slipped into the room, wearing a black dress coat and white cravat. Introductions were made, and as Granville pulled another chair near to his desk, he expanded on the duties of his comrade.

"Mr. Hurst is the Librarian of the Bank, but not to be confused with the sort of librarian with which you may be more familiar. His duties have nothing to do with books whatsoever."

"Indeed." My curiosity was most definitely piqued. "Then if I might be so bold as to enquire, Mr. Hurst, what are the duties of a librarian with no books?"

"It's really quite simple," Hurst replied as he favoured me with a glance that revealed penetrating green eyes. "I am responsible for notes that have been paid in at the bank. Once they come to me, they are completely devoid of value, but we must keep track of them and preserve them should a claim of forgery or theft arise. After a suitable period of time they are burned, which is an absolute necessity, as fresh bundles and parcels of notes arrive every day and reach almost to the ceiling."

"Most interesting," observed Holmes. "Now then, down to business. Tell us more about this Amateur Mendicant Society and your concerns."

Before either gentleman could say a word, the door to the office opened and a clerk brought in a tray with four small glasses filled with an amber-coloured liquid.

"Ah, excellent!" said Granville. "A touch of sherry makes everything a bit more civilised."

In turn, the clerk offered each of us a glass, then retreated as silently as he had come. Granville raised his glass and we all followed suit.

"To your very good health, gentlemen!"

Sipping my sherry and savouring the warm, nutty taste as I once more gazed around the room, it was easy to feel in that moment that I was at the very centre of civilisation. Granville looked at his glass with appreciation, then set it down and turned his attention to the matter at hand.

"Might I enquire if either of you gentlemen are familiar with the origin of the Mendicants within the Catholic Church?"

"I have a passing knowledge," answered Holmes. "I believe it was the Second Council of Lyon in 1274 that established the four main orders: The Franciscans, the Carmelites, the Dominicans, and the Augustinians."

"Quite right, Mr. Holmes," Granville nodded his approval. "Up until that point, the various religious orders had focused on staying in one place, often perfecting a particular trade, and gradually accumulating land, buildings, and considerable wealth. The Mendicants, in contrast, had no property or possessions beyond that which they carried with them, and travelled from place to place as itinerant preachers. Theirs was a lifestyle of poverty and sacrifice, dedicated entirely to spreading the Word of God to all the world."

Mr. Hurst had followed this disquisition closely, and as he put his sherry glass down, he proceeded to enlighten us further. "Human nature being what it is, tensions soon arose between the so-called 'begging friars' and their religious brethren who preferred a more, shall we say, comfortable lifestyle. In my experience, there are chiefly two branches of humanity, those who seek to do everything they can to benefit themselves and those who seek to do everything they can to benefit others. The humble and ascetic lifestyle of the mendicants was a repudiation of the wealth and splendour of the Vatican. Thus the mendicants came to be seen as a threat by the powers that be, with the result that the more rigorous mendicant orders found themselves suppressed by various popes down through the years, and many went extinct."

"Which brings us to our own little society, the Amateur Mendicants," declared Granville. "We are dedicated to the principles of the original mendicants, but with no religious associations whatsoever. Whatever funds or goods we are able to gather go entirely to the poor and needy. Our name is simply a little joke, nothing more. However, it would appear that our mission and sense of humour isn't entirely appreciated by everyone."

With that, Granville withdrew a small slip of paper from his pocket, and Hurst did the same. As they set both pieces of paper on the desk, Holmes and I could see that they were almost identical, and bore the same words:

The Amateur Mendicant Society must be disbanded immediately. Ignore this warning at your peril.

Holmes picked up one of the notes, then the other, holding them both up to the light, smelling them, then comparing them next to one another.

"Both the paper and ink are unexceptional," Holmes announced, "and they would appear to be written by the same hand, but the individual letters themselves were slowly and laboriously composed, indicating the writer was attempting to disguise any identifying features of his own handwriting. How did you come by these?"

"They were delivered by post four days ago," answered Granville, setting a torn envelope on the desk, with Hurst doing the same.

After a cursory glance at both envelopes, Holmes leaned back in his chair. "Anything else?"

Granville and Hurst flickered a glance at one another, and it was Granville who spoke first.

"After receiving the warning, as you might expect, I was alert to any other possible threats, and came to feel that I was being followed on my way to and from the bank. Normally, my mind is on business, and I take very little note of passersby or other people in my vicinity, but by stopping abruptly and turning on numerous occasions, I began to feel quite certain that I was being pursued by two priests."

"Priests?" I asked in surprise.

"I wish I could be more specific," continued Granville, "but they never approached closely enough for a more accurate description. I may, of course, be fabricating this out of my own imagination. You know how it is. You pay no mind to chimney sweeps for most of your life, but then you see or read something about chimney sweeps and suddenly you find the streets are positively swimming with them."

"Mr. Hurst?" Holmes turned to the bank's librarian. "Did you notice anything similar?"

Hurst nodded. "Once Trevor mentioned that he was being followed, I began to be more mindful of my surroundings, and yes, I feel quite certain that I am being watched."

"By priests?" asked Holmes.

"Possibly," answered Hurst warily. "Or at least gentlemen wearing priestly garb. It's most unsettling. I am used to living my life and conducting my affairs on an almost completely anonymous basis. I have never sought out attention and I never shall. It isn't in my nature. I am a private man. To suddenly find myself the object of unwanted attention is distressing in the extreme."

"My colleague's distress is my own," said Granville, "and so I wrote to you, Mr. Holmes, in the hope that you might be able to shed some light on the situation. To disband the Amateur Mendicant Society based on nothing more than a threatening note doesn't sit well with me, and yet having the proverbial Sword of Damocles hanging over our heads is most definitely worrisome."

"Especially considering this evening," added Hurst.

Holmes looked quizzically from Hurst to Granville, who folded his hands in front of him and gazed at Holmes and me in turn.

"Tonight is the occasion of our annual dinner," began Granville. "The Amateur Mendicants gather together in very humble surroundings to enjoy the most lavish feast imaginable. It's our little gift to ourselves, you might say, and encourages continued participation within the Society."

"Given that," Hurst picked up the story, "in discussing the matter, it seems obvious that if someone were looking to inflict some kind of harm or mischief upon us, this would be the ideal opportunity, as it is the only time of the year when we are all gathered in one place."

Holmes took all this in, his mind instantly assembling together the pieces of this remarkable story to come to a logical conclusion. "You have made your position quite clear. Dr. Watson and I would be happy to attend your dinner this evening."

Granville and Hurst looked at one another in surprise.

"Well, yes," said Granville. "That is precisely what we were about to propose."

"Of course, we wouldn't introduce you by name," continued Hurst. "We would simply note that you were prospective new members. Should any unpleasantness arise, it would no doubt be to our advantage to have you and Dr. Watson on the premises."

Holmes rose from his seat and began making a tour of the room, stopping before a particularly magnificent urn featuring Hercules doing battle against the Hydra as one of his Twelve Labours.

"I take it," said Holmes, "that you are concerned not only about threats from without, but also from within."

With his back to us, Holmes couldn't see the furtive glance exchanged between Hurst and Granville.

"A slim possibility," acknowledged Granville, "but one that we must bear in mind. Ours is a Society of quite exceptional gentlemen, each used to having his way and manipulating circumstances to his own benefit. It would be fatuous to declare otherwise."

"But surely," I expostulated, "if any of these gentlemen should disapprove of some aspect of the Society, they could simply resign their membership."

"Which would raise uncomfortable questions," answered Hurst. "The slightest ripple in this particular pond is a cause for alarm, because it indicates more powerful currents running beneath the surface."

"To the public eye," Holmes had rejoined us, "there is nothing to connect seemingly disparate industries, noble families, and departments of the government. However, they are all part of one web, and a tremor in this part of the web can result in cataclysmic consequences elsewhere."

"Well put," agreed Granville. "You have a nice understanding of things, Mr. Holmes, and I feel certain we can rely on your abilities and discretion to put this current unpleasantness behind us."

"Is there anything else I should know?" asked Holmes.

"Yes," answered Granville. "In a further effort to bring everything out into the open, we have invited two members of the Diocese of Westminster to join us this evening."

"The Professional Mendicant Society, as it were," added Hurst with a wry smile. "Our fundraising activities pale in comparison to theirs."

"But if the threats against us are simply their way of demanding money," concluded Granville, "we will simply buy them off with a superb dinner and a donation to their coffers."

Our conference with these two gentlemen concluded shortly thereafter, and Holmes eschewed a cab in favour of walking back to Baker Street. We proceeded in silence for some time, and it was only as we passed Chancery Lane that Holmes emerged from his musings to cast a glance at the leaden sky above us.

"What is it that's troubling you?" I asked.

"Everything," he answered. "Typically, powerful men and powerful institutions make it their business to tilt the game to their advantage and to wreak havoc on the classes below them. For the most part, there is an unspoken agreement that certain activities and territories are inviolate, and it is in this way that the Church, the government, and our captains of industry can blame our various social ills on whomever they please: immigrants, Socialists, the Jews, the Irish, and so on. However, if two of these forces should come into direct conflict – for example, the Church and the Bank of England – there is no telling the amount of damage they could do to the country."

"Good Heavens!" I was genuinely taken aback by what Holmes was saying. "Does the situation really appear that dire?"

"Difficult to say. Human nature being what it is, it may resolve itself down to nothing more than a personal grudge. Still, I think we would both do well to arm ourselves for this evening's adventure. It is a wise man who anticipates and a foolish man who reacts."

I will admit that I passed the rest of the day in a bit of a haze, wandering from this book to that periodical, but all the while with my mind racing ahead to what events might unfold that evening. Holmes was unusually quiet, smoking pipe after pipe, with only occasional forays into this or that volume of his Index to verify some point of information. Darkness had fallen by the time that he abruptly announced, "I do believe our presence is requested."

A moment later I heard a knock on our door and we proceeded down the stairs to the carriage that had been prearranged for us. Upon entering the carriage, I immediately noted that smoked windows prevented us from looking out, just as they prevented anyone else from looking in. About to voice an objection, a terse shake of Holmes's head silenced the words in my throat, and I sat across from him with my heart rate already accelerating. The ensuing journey took over half-an-hour, although I couldn't determine just how far we had actually travelled. For all I knew, we had done nothing more than move in an enormous circle, so that we may very well have ended up several miles away or merely a street away from Baker Street.

As the horses slowed, I could see Holmes's eyes darting back and forth, listening to anything that might give us a clue as to our location. When the carriage door was opened, Holmes and I descended into an alleyway outside a rather unremarkable warehouse which loomed forebodingly above us in the dim gaslight. As our carriage clattered off into the distance, I heard a low, mournful ship horn sounding on the Thames, and pulled my coat tighter.

"This can't be right," I began. "Devilish sort of place for a dinner party."

Holmes nodded. "Then let us see what form of devilry awaits us within."

As we approached the building, a door swung upon, anticipating our arrival, and a doorman appeared and beckoned us towards him. A moment later we were inside the warehouse and descending one flight of stairs after another, my unease increasing with every step. Feeling my trusty Webley by my side was the only thing that calmed my nerves as we reached the basement of the building and proceeded down a bleak, cheerless corridor. A door at the end of it was opened, and upon stepping through it was as if Holmes and I had entered a different universe. A large, capacious room was filled with golden light, a string quartet was encamped in one of the corners providing music, and a roaring fire welcomed all weary and cold travellers. I quickly ascertained that the long dining table in the centre of the room was positively groaning with all manner of culinary delights, and estimated that approximately twenty gentlemen were already sitting at the table, at the far end of which sat both Granville and Hurst, flanked by two men wearing simple clerical vestments.

Granville rose from his place at our appearance. "Welcome, gentlemen, welcome! We're so glad that you're able to join us. Please, take your seats, and let the yearly dinner of the Amateur Mendicant Society commence!"

Holmes and I had no sooner settled into our places than a dozen servers appeared out of nowhere and began filling our plates with anything that we desired. There was glazed ham, roasted goose, lamb with cold mint sauce, broiled brook trout, *au gratin* potatoes, all manner of delectably prepared root vegetables, fruit of every description, sweetmeats, and so forth. A palate cleanser of chartreuse sherbet appeared halfway through this feast, then the table was liberally festooned with camembert and Roquefort cheeses, as well as crystallised ginger, Tunis dates, and table figs. As much as I tried to keep my wits about me, the siren song of this sumptuous banquet had lulled me into a kind of daze, when I was suddenly brought back to reality by Granville tapping insistently on the side of his glass with a spoon.

"Gentlemen! If I might have your attention please, a delicious Italian amaretto from Saronno has been procured for your delectation and will now be served. The lights will then be extinguished for our final and most spectacular course of the evening. Following that, I shall announce the various bequests of the Amateur Mendicant Society for the upcoming Year of our Lord, 1888."

In short order, every glass was filled with amaretto, and then the room was pitched into complete darkness before I observed two glowing blue balls of fire approaching. It was an eerie, exhilarating sight, as what I immediately recognised as two Christmas puddings doused with brandy and then lit on fire apparently levitated on their own through the room. By the time they were set on the table, the brandy had almost burned off, the lights came on again, and we all spontaneously applauded this remarkable and memorable demonstration.

Granville rose from his chair, raised his glass, and addressed the gathering.

"A toast, gentlemen, to the Amateur Mendicant Society, to our members, to our deeds, and to this quite delectable dinner. Cheers!"

As one, we raised our glasses and drank. When Granville flamboyantly tossed his glass into the fire, we all followed suit with a rousing cheer. Granville then proceeded to produce a paper from his pocket, unfolded it, and put on a pair of spectacles to read what I supposed were the newest recipients of the largesse of the Amateur Mendicant Society. However, instead of reading, his face took on a shocked expression and he began to wheeze audibly, struggling for breath. To his side, Hurst was already clawing at his own throat, his eyes bulging from their sockets as his entire body twisted in agony. Mere seconds later, both men had collapsed to the floor and in the ensuing panic the room was soon cleared of all of its inhabitants – save for Holmes and myself.

Even as I knelt by Hurst, a terrible death rattle emerged from him as he took his last breath and fell still, while Granville writhed on the floor, froth streaming from his lips. I attempted to force open his jaw, with the intent of thrusting my fingers down his throat to induce vomiting, but he struggled and convulsed so violently that I was unable to do so. Endeavouring to control his thrashing to the best of my ability, I saw that Holmes was bending over the still form of Hurst, sniffing at the dead man's lips.

"What is it?" I asked.

Holmes turned to me. "A distinct odour of bitter almonds, which one would expect from a man who just consumed a glass of amaretto, but also consistent with the odour of prussic acid, otherwise known as hydrogen cyanide."

Granville's contortions had slowed, and a low moan escaped him. I saw his eyes open and a flicker of humanity behind them. He was still alive, at any rate, and Holmes sent me off to fetch the police and medical help as he stayed behind to monitor Granville's health and to more closely investigate the scene of the crime. In due course, the police arrived and Holmes related everything that had transpired to Inspector Lestrade of Scotland Yard, as Granville was taken away to Barts Hospital, and the covered form of the late Mr. Hurst was conveyed to the mortuary. It was close to three hours later that Holmes and I dragged ourselves back to Baker Street and I immediately fell into bed and a deep sleep.

When I awoke, it took me a moment or two to orient myself. At first, I imagined that the events of the previous night had simply been a nightmare, but then, as a greater sense of consciousness asserted itself, the whole hideous sequence of events played itself out in my memory with disturbing clarity. Dragging myself to my feet, I made my way to our sitting room, where I encountered what I can only describe as a veritable London pea-souper. The room was utterly suffused in smoke, with Holmes at the centre of it, still puffing on his pipe. Despite the frigid temperature outside, I opened a window, gulped in several lungfuls of brisk December air, then turned back inside.

"What the devil, Holmes?" I enquired. "Have you been sitting here smoking since we came back from the Amateur Mendicant Society?"

"What do you make of it?" answered Holmes, ignoring my question. "I would value your opinion of last night's tragic events."

"It seems perfectly obvious to me," I replied. "The priests sitting next to Granville and Hurst poisoned both of them!"

"A bold claim," returned Holmes, "and one devoid of any meaningful details. Can you be more specific?"

"Holmes, you saw everything as well as I did. The amaretto was poured into each man's empty glass. The lights were then extinguished so that we might better focus on the arrival of the flaming Christmas puddings. It was in that moment of darkness that one or both of the priests took the opportunity to introduce prussic acid into the glasses of both Granville and Hurst. Once they drained their glasses, it took a moment or two for the poison to take effect, following which Hurst passed away almost immediately, and Granville barely survived."

"Indeed," Holmes rose from his chair to walk to the window. "Does it strike you as odd that Hurst died so quickly and yet Granville is still alive?"

"Not particularly," I replied. "For one thing, Granville weighs at least twice as much as Hurst, so the poison would affect Hurst all the more rapidly. Or perhaps there was a larger dose of the prussic acid in his glass."

"Perfectly logical," Holmes nodded. "And yet, while we were both encouraged to see an elaborate conspiracy unfolding before our eyes, I suspect that a much more simple crime took place."

"How so?"

"If I might put it in somewhat poetic terms, I would call it the curious case of the absence of grace."

"Pardon?"

"I would expect any dinner with two priests in attendance as special guests to include the saying of grace before the meal. Failing that, I would expect the two priests to say a quiet grace between themselves. Neither of those events occurred."

"What are you suggesting?" I asked.

"Let us forge the logical chain that might proceed from this observation," began Holmes. "The two priests neglected to say grace. Therefore, we must consider the possibility that they weren't actually priests, but merely actors playing the role of clergymen. But why? To what end? Well, Granville had planted the seed in our minds that the Amateur Mendicant Society was being threatened by the Church. He claimed that he was being followed by clergymen."

"And Hurst said the very same thing!" I added.

"So he did. I would suspect by the same actors who arrived at the dinner."

"But why all this subterfuge?"

"Quite simple," answered Holmes. "Because Mr. Granville wished to murder Mr. Hurst and to have the blame placed elsewhere – specifically, on two mysterious figures who would disappear as quickly as they had appeared. The police would be on the hunt for two clergymen who never existed."

"Holmes!" I cried. "Are you forgetting that Granville very nearly lost his own life?"

Holmes arched his eyebrows in response. "Did he?"

"You saw him yourself! He was in spasms of agony!"

"Was he?"

My mind was in a whirl. Was Holmes simply having a bit of fun at my expense? But surely this was too horrible a situation to treat so lightly.

"Holmes," I began, "please explain yourself."

Knocking a dottle of tobacco from his pipe, Holmes proceeded to sit in his armchair and steepled his fingers together.

"I suspect something along the following lines: Mr. Granville likes money. He is surrounded by the world of high finance. His not-inconsiderable collection of Greek pottery would require sizable amounts of capital to amass, because the Panathenaic amphorae that I inspected all appear to be authentic originals. He quite literally has a painting of King Croesus above his desk, and you may take it from me, a wealthy man who declares that money isn't everything is lying through his teeth.

"Any salary from the Bank of England would scarcely meet his requirements, so he began to augment his income in a variety of not entirely ethical or legal ways. When this still proved insufficient, he conjured up the concept of the Amateur Mendicant Society out of thin air and enlisted the aid of his colleague, Mr. Hurst, to give the whole enterprise a patina of greater respectability. I don't doubt that some of the funds gathered by the Society made their way to the poor and needy, but I suspect that a considerable portion of that money made its way into Mr. Granville's pockets.

"All it would take is a bit of accounting legerdemain to obscure his nefarious activities, but here we must bear in mind the expertise of Mr. Hurst, who specialises in keeping track of financial affairs. Something regarding the accounts of the Amateur Mendicant Society aroused his suspicions to the extent that he expressed his concerns to Mr. Granville. This, of course, would never do, especially should Mr. Hurst's suspicions lead him to other enquiries at the Bank of England. And so, the plot was hatched in Mr. Granville's brain.

"Threatening notes were produced. Actors to portray priests were hired. You and I were brought in as witnesses of impeccable reputation. Amaretto was served instead of port to provide the odour of almonds so that the smell of his own breath and that of Mr. Hurst would be virtually identical. The lights were doused, Mr. Granville surreptitiously introduced prussic acid into Mr. Hurst's glass, and then the amaretto was consumed. Mr. Granville grandly tossed his glass into the fireplace to obscure the fact that there was never any prussic acid in it, with the rest of us following suit. He then had to merely feign violent illness, while his colleague died a horrible death not ten feet away."

I sat down heavily, still taking in everything Holmes had said. "Well, if what you're saying is correct, what can we do?" I began. "Should we try and get the books of the Amateur Mendicant Society?"

"I suspect they are nonexistent," answered Holmes. "Mr. Granville would have seen to that prior to last night's dinner."

"Then the Bank of England," I suggested. "Perhaps more concrete proof can be found there."

"Perhaps," agreed Holmes. "But then we are in the world of larceny or embezzlement, not murder, and a respected gentleman like Mr. Granville would most likely be let off with a gentle tap on the wrist so as not to draw attention to his crimes, which would alarm the general public and undermine the reputation of the Bank."

"Then he gets away with it?" I asked. "Committing cold-blooded murder under our very noses? Surely we can do something?"

"That is what I have been mulling over these past few hours – considering what tactics we might take in this quite remarkable case."

"And?"

"I suggest the following very speculative plan," said Holmes. "Let me contact Lestrade at Scotland Yard and ask him to meet us at Barts. We'll arrange a private conference with Mr. Granville and see what sort of condition he is in. I suspect he'll be feigning some kind of after-effects of the poison, so we'll consult with a doctor as to his prognosis. I would simply ask you, Watson, to be alert to any direction the conversation may take. Whatever I say, no matter how outlandish it might sound, please agree with me immediately. If Mr. Granville can concoct a charade for our benefit, it's only fair that we should return the favour."

It was three hours later that Holmes and I were walking down a corridor in Barts, accompanied by a young, nervous doctor, who couldn't have been more than a year or two out of university. As we approached Granville's room, I saw Lestrade lurking in the hallway, where Holmes had clearly told him to wait for us. Approaching Lestrade, Holmes spoke in low tones.

"Notebook out, Lestrade," directed Holmes. "Not a word once we step into this room. Watch, listen, and you may hear something to your advantage."

As a group, we all filed into Granville's room, where the patient was sitting up in bed, looking somewhat apprehensive, but none the worse for wear.

"My dear Granville," began Holmes solicitously, even going so far as to take the man's hand in his own. "How are you feeling?"

"A little shaken, Mr. Holmes," answered Granville. "It has been quite the ordeal. Poor Hurst!"

"Indeed," Holmes nodded. "And how is your stomach? It isn't every man that can take a dose of prussic acid and survive."

"Unsettled, to be sure."

"I can imagine. Ingesting prussic acid can result in violent cramping for up to two days after the event. Were you able to sleep, at all? Are the spasms tolerable?"

Granville's mouth twisted in a slight grimace, "I don't like to complain, Mr. Holmes."

"Have they offered you anything for the pain?"

As Granville shook his head, Holmes whirled on the doctor standing behind him. "What's the meaning of this? Do you have any idea of the agony this poor man must be in? I once witnessed a man clawing the flesh off the back of his own hands due to a mild dose of prussic acid. My colleague, Dr. Watson, treated countless men on the battlefields of Afghanistan. Let me ask you, Watson, was it typically your habit to let soldiers suffer the tortures of the damned when they had been wounded?"

"Good God, no!" I retorted. "That's what morphine is for. My job was to alleviate suffering, not prolong it."

Holmes turned to the doctor, his eyes blazing. "I demand an explanation!"

The poor doctor was so overwhelmed by Holmes's imperious manner and my comments regarding my wartime experience that he immediately fled the room. Lestrade was frantically jotting something down in his notebook as Holmes paced briefly, and then a moment later the doctor was back with a syringe of morphine. As it was injected into a vein in Granville's arm, he immediately settled back onto his pillows with a serene and glazed expression.

"Excellent!" Holmes looked at Granville approvingly. "That's better, isn't it?"

Granville managed a nod and even a small smile as the sedating effects of the morphine coursed through his system.

"Then we won't trouble you any further, Mr. Granville," continued Holmes, "but I would be grateful if you could answer one question. Why did you wish to kill Mr. Hurst?"

"What's that?" mumbled Granville, an expression of shock slowly spreading over his features.

"I watched you do it," answered Holmes. "The lights were doused, the room went dark, and you poured prussic acid into Mr. Hurst's glass."

"No..." Granville faltered, fighting through the fog in his brain. "The lights were doused...there was no light to see...no light..."

"Ah, I should explain," continued Holmes affably. "I am afflicted with a rather rare condition in which my eyes do not require the usual length of time to adjust to the dark. It has proved invaluable in at least two of our cases, hasn't it, Watson?"

"I should say so," I replied, mindful of Holmes's instruction that I should agree with everything he said. "'*Retinal homeostasis,*' as it's known. Quite rare indeed."

"Which allowed me to watch you pour the prussic acid into Mr. Hurst's glass as clearly as I see you now, Mr. Granville. I can only assume, therefore, that he must have threatened you in some way."

It would be impossible to describe with any accuracy the emotions that swept across Granville's features as Holmes's words penetrated his opiate-addled brain. Holmes had said everything with such certainty and conviction, that the idea of contradicting him in any way must have seemed impossible. All recollection that he was supposed to be suffering from prussic acid poisoning himself had been utterly effaced from his memory.

"He..." Granville tried to wrench his thoughts into place. "It was the damned bookkeeping...poking his nose where it didn't belong. Numbers...I knew he was poking his nose...the Mendicants...questions at the bank. We're talking ruin, Mr.

Holmes...absolute ruin...I couldn't bear it...only a matter of time unless...it's a bad business to be sure...but it couldn't be helped...couldn't be helped..."

Granville lapsed into a groggy silence, and as I glanced at Lestrade I observed his mouth quite literally hanging open.

"And with that," said Holmes, "I leave the case in your capable hands, Lestrade."

Holmes was out the door in an instant, his long strides taking him down the corridor as both the doctor and Lestrade ran after him. It was the doctor who caught up to Holmes first.

"Mr. Holmes! I must object! To drug a patient and then induce a confession out of him is most irregular."

"The ends justify the means," replied Holmes tersely, "and it was you who administered the morphine, not I. Besides, the man was still in some emotional distress following the excitement of last night, and a little morphine can have an agreeably settling influence. I speak from personal experience."

"The doctor is quite right." Lestrade had finally caught up with Holmes. "You can't drug a suspect to interrogate them."

"Perhaps your position precludes such a tactic," answered Holmes, "but you will recall that I am not a member of the police force, nor am I a physician. I merely made the point that morphine is used to alleviate suffering. What followed was entirely out of my hands, and I hope you took accurate notes of Mr. Granville's statement. I might add that an audit of the Bank of England's books might prove edifying and, to the best of my knowledge, prussic acid isn't in the inventory of most shopkeepers, so where did he procure it? Good day, gentlemen!"

As Holmes and I rode in our hansom back to Baker Street, a light snow had begun to fall and with a jolt of recognition I remembered that tomorrow was Christmas Day. I had fully intended to present Holmes with a new cherry-wood pipe in the morning, but recent events had prevented my intended visit to a tobacconist's. Happily enough, I spotted such a shop just ahead of us and inspiration struck.

"I say," I began, "perhaps I'll just get out and walk back to Baker Street. I fancy stretching my legs a bit."

Holmes turned to me with a quizzical expression, but one that quickly turned to bemusement as his gaze turned to the street and he spotted the tobacconist's shop.

"Very thoughtful, Watson, but you have already given me the finest Christmas present possible."

"I have?"

"'*Retinal homeostasis,*'" replied Holmes with a low chuckle. "Quite wonderful. I knew I could count on you and your powers of invention."

"Thank you, Holmes," I answered, a feeling of warmth and pride welling up in me.

"Thank you, old friend. Now then, I must confess that I found my appetite keenly whetted last night before events took a dark turn. Given that, it is absolutely imperative that we embark on our next mystery immediately: Where to find a Christmas pudding?"

The year '87 furnished us with a long series of cases of greater or less interest, of which I retain the records. Among my headings under this one twelve months I find an account of the adventure...of the Amateur Mendicant Society, who held a luxurious club in the lower vault of a furniture warehouse...

– Dr. John Watson
"The Five Orange Pips"

Death of a Mudlark

"Mudlarking" on the banks of the River Thames is an activity that goes back centuries. Thanks to the strong, scouring tides of the river, all manner of objects are dredged up from the riverbed and deposited on the banks, where enterprising individuals of all persuasions may happen upon any number of bizarre and curious items ranging from clay pipes to Roman coins. Competition for the best hunting grounds can be fierce, and when a young boy is murdered simply for being in the wrong place at the wrong time, Holmes and Watson venture forth to do some hunting of their own.

It will not come as an earth-shattering revelation to my readers for me to declare that living in close proximity to another human being means that over the course of time, we are increasingly able to accurately gauge their mood and general frame of mind without a single word being uttered. This was most assuredly the case with my good friend Sherlock Holmes who, for all of his considerable gifts, did not include concealing his feelings among them. Or to be more accurate, his inclination to conceal his state of mind within the cosy confines of our rooms at 221b Baker Street was minimal. As one might judge the weather by a drop in the barometric pressure, one could measure the days he had been without a case by the degree of chaos to be observed in our living quarters. This was usually accompanied by spontaneous grunts or growls of general dissatisfaction, and long periods spent looking out our window with his hands thrust deeply into the pockets of his dressing gown.

In the late spring of 1894, a full week had passed since any client or official representative of the police had called upon us, and only small patches of our floor were visible amongst the sea of scattered newspapers that Holmes had flung this way or that after a perfunctory reading. It was a delicate business landing upon a conversational salvo that wouldn't be met with either silence or pointed sarcasm, but at length Holmes's dark mood became a boil needing to be lanced, and as both his friend and a member of the medical profession, I knew it was my duty to execute the unpleasant task. Bracing myself as he stood at the window looking out at the gathering dusk, I addressed Holmes's back in what I hoped was a pleasant and carefree manner.

"Looks to be a pleasant day tomorrow," I began. "What do you say to a stroll through Hyde Park? Get a bit of fresh air."

With no response immediately forthcoming, I gathered my reserves and pressed on. "Or perhaps the British Museum? Don't they have a new exhibit on display? Something or other about whales?"

At this, Holmes turned and came a step or two toward me, kicking at a crumpled up edition of *The Times*. "You and I both know that it's ridiculous. Perfectly ridiculous. And no stroll through Hyde Park or museum display featuring our cetacean friends will make it any less ridiculous. We live in a city with some six million inhabitants, and you mean to tell me that in the past week there has been no crime or mystery worthy of my attention? Not one? Absurd."

"You haven't seen anything to pique your interest in the newspapers?" I enquired.

"Hints here and there," answered Holmes. "Whiffs of various forms of malfeasance. A fire at a haberdashery that was most certainly arson, the pilfering of three furs from a shop in the Strand, no fewer than six unexplained deaths, three outside pubs in Whitechapel – two in the vicinity of Trafalgar Square, and one not fifty yards from the Thames – yet neither the police nor anyone else has been inclined to seek my advice or assistance. And here another day has come and gone, and nothing. Nothing..."

Holmes trailed off, and just as I was pondering the possibility of embarking upon a crime spree myself to give him a case to work on, I heard the downstairs door open with force, a cry of surprise from Mrs. Hudson, and then footsteps pounding up the steps to our rooms. When our door was flung open it was a young, pale-faced boy who stood there, panic and exhaustion in his features, with his clothes and hands covered in greyish mud. Right behind him was Mrs. Hudson, uttering all manner of cries of distress at the appearance of this filthy intruder, but Holmes merely waved her away, closed the door, and then directed his full attention to our visitor.

"Why, it's Bisset, isn't it?" declared Holmes.

With a nod, the young man confirmed his identity, and then with a rush of movement he ran to our window to scan the street below before turning back to us. It was no great feat to read the fear and agitation in his expression. I had little doubt that he had just been running for his life, and now, instead of making any kind of remark, he opened up a clenched fist to reveal what appeared to be a sizable emerald in the palm of his hand. Its green colour stood out all the more radiantly given the grey mud caking his skin, and Holmes plucked the jewel from him and held it up to the light. Turning it this way and that, Holmes flashed a glance in my direction, then addressed the boy.

"I want you clean yourself up, compose yourself, and I will have Mrs. Hudson prepare you some food. At that point, I would be most interested in hearing how this object happened to come into your possession. Would that be agreeable to you?"

At a nod from the young man, Holmes ushered him in the direction of some soap and water, then handed me the jewel before venturing downstairs to give instructions to Mrs. Hudson. When he returned, I was still gazing at the sizable emerald with some disbelief. Opening a drawer in his desk and removing a magnifying lens, Holmes took the gem from me and proceeded to examine it closely under a strong light.

"It can't be real," I offered. "It must be glass. A genuine emerald of that size…"

"I do note some imperfections in it," began Holmes. "A tiny crack here, for example."

"Well, there you are, then," I said. "It's a fake."

"To the contrary," Holmes continued to turn the gem in his fingers. "Real emeralds typically contain flaws of some kind, or what are known as *inclusions*. It is when a stone appears to be perfect that it is usually a fake. The colour of this stone is ideal, what an enthusiast might call a 'velvety' green. The weight feels correct as well – that is, it's heavier than an object of this size made of glass. I would put it at about twelve carats, and with its classic emerald cut, a truly first-rate example of the gem."

Taking to his armchair, Holmes tented his fingers and looked at me.

"Well, what do you make of it?"

"If what you say is true," I began, "if this a genuine emerald, it must be worth a small fortune."

"I concur," answered Holmes.

"And you know this boy?" I asked.

"I do. He has been of use to me on no fewer than three occasions as part of the Baker Street Irregulars. Quite excellent when it comes to following people that I wish to have followed. But this…" Holmes gazed into the heart of the jewel. "…this takes young Mr. Bisset into very deep waters indeed. We may assume that he hasn't stolen it, because he would scarcely come here if that were the case. However, it has somehow come into his possession, and that possession has put him in fear of his life. It is that fear which has brought him here, as presumably he has nowhere else to turn."

In short order, Mrs. Hudson brought up some tea and sandwiches, and a few moments later, a somewhat cleaner and calmer Bisset entered our sitting room. Holmes waved him toward the food, and the young man did not require a second invitation, immediately tucking into a ham sandwich and availing himself liberally of the biscuits which Mrs. Hudson had been thoughtful enough to include.

"You have had an evening of some excitement, Bisset," observed Holmes.

"I should say so, sir," answered the young man, taking a healthy gulp of tea. "And not the kind of excitement I am anxious to repeat."

"How did this gem happen to come into your possession?"

"Luck, sir," answered the boy. "Pure, blind luck. At first, I assumed it to be good luck, but my opinion on that score changed quickly."

Getting up from his chair, Holmes packed some tobacco into his cherry-wood pipe, lit it, then sat back down as the boy continued to gorge himself.

"Please do your best to describe the sequence of events as clearly as you can. Omit nothing."

"I'll do my best, sir." Bisset turned his chair toward Holmes, who had now closed his eyes. "Are you familiar at all with mudlarking?"

Holmes nodded. "Scavenging on the banks of the Thames."

"Right you are, sir," answered Bisset. "If you venture down there after the tide has gone out, there's no telling what manner of things you are likely to come across. Clothing, old clay pipes, coins, dead animals, even the odd dead person. People throw themselves off bridges or lose their way after a night in the pubs or opium dens, and if you happen to get stuck in the mud as the tide is coming back in – well, that's the end of you. I do my best scavenging at either dawn or dusk, because the angle of the sun hits anything metal and you can see the shine."

"Interesting strategy," I remarked as I scrawled down some notes. "It's quite remarkable that the pickings from the river replenish themselves on a daily basis."

Holmes opened his eyes. "The tidal pull on the Thames is a very powerful one, practically scouring the riverbed every day, with the result that all manner of objects, both ancient and modern, may find themselves deposited on the banks in full view of anyone with enough enterprise to come along and pick them up. Given that, mudlarking can provide a meagre income for the adolescent boys whose youthful nimbleness and light

115

frames allow them to skip to and fro across the slick surface. How long have you been at this, Bisset?"

"Almost a year now, sir. Some of the bigger lads can be a bit territorial, but as they get older and slower, they move on to some other enterprise. I do all right. I like the excitement of it, never knowing what might turn up. Just last month I picked up a Roman coin, neat as you please, sitting there like Julius Caesar himself had dropped it. Took it to a dealer and got two quid for it."

"And what happened this evening?"

"I was out at my usual time, down by Wapping Pier, but a bit nervous to be honest, because of what happened to Dickie Bentham just a few days ago."

Holmes looked up sharply. "Dickie Bentham, you say? He was most useful to me in the Keown case. Do you happen to recall that sordid affair, Watson?"

"All too vividly," I replied, with an involuntary shudder.

Holmes returned his attention to Bisset. "What happened to Dickie?"

"He's dead, Mr. Holmes."

A flash of emotion crossed Holmes's features. "I'm sorry to hear that. Very sorry, indeed. There was a rather perfunctory article in the paper that said a drowning victim had been found, but no name was given."

"Drowning victim," repeated Bisset. "You'd drown too if some great lummox was holding your head in the river."

"Start from the beginning," instructed Holmes.

"It was Dickie's first time mudlarking," said Bisset. "He was a bit young and not keen on the water, but then he saw some of the things me and the other lads were finding. He asked if he could come with me, so we went down there together…" Bisset paused, the memory of events overwhelming him. "It was my fault what happened."

"How so?" asked Holmes.

"I never warned him, see?" continued the boy. "When you find something, you don't make a fuss. You keep your mouth shut and slip into your pocket or a bag. So, Dickie's down a bit from me, maybe a hundred yards or so. I'm minding my own business, about to pack it in because the sun has just gone down, and then I hear this yelping coming from Dickie. I look his way and he's waving his hand in the air like he's found a sovereign in the mud. As he heads back to dry land, I see these two big blokes heading his way, with an even bigger bloke standing well back…Big Jamie."

"You know this man?" asked Holmes.

"Know enough to avoid him," answered Bisset. "Complete nutter from Glasgow. He's got razors sewn inside the lapels of his coat in case anyone tries to grab him and only half an ear from a knife fight. He's shouting directions to his men, and when they get to Dickie they start throwing him back and forth like a doll, tearing the clothes off him, searching for whatever he's found. When they find it, they head back to Big Jamie and hand him something. He looks at it, waves those two away, then goes down to where Dickie is and pushes him face down into the mud, then holds him there until he stops moving. It was horrible."

By this point I had had the good sense to bring out my notebook to record this story, and I paused in my writing, "And what did the police say when you reported it?"

As both Holmes and young Bisset looked at me in mystification, I immediately realised my error. Young gentlemen of Bisset's class made it a practise to avoid any and all contact with the constabulary, regardless of what crime has been committed. I returned my attention to my notebook as Holmes addressed Bisset.

"And yet despite the crime that you witnessed, you made the decision to return to the spot where Dickie had been murdered."

"Yes, sir," answered Bisset. "Whatever he found, it was something valuable. And you know how it is, if there's one thing, well then, maybe there's something else worthwhile nearby. Sure enough, after an hour or so of poking around, I saw this flash of green and picked it up. Just as I was splashing some water on it to get a better look, I see these two blokes heading in my direction, and I see Big Jamie standing further up the bank. I didn't want to end up like poor Dickie, so I scarpered right quick and managed to get away from them. I couldn't go to the police and there's no one else I can trust, so I came straight here, Mr. Holmes. You've always been more than decent to me, and you always seem to know what to do in, well, peculiar situations."

Holmes offered a thin smile. "You're too kind, my boy. But yes, I do specialise in, as you call them, 'peculiar situations,' of which this is most definitely one." Holmes paused, his grey eyes shifting pensively before returning his full attention to the boy. "Would you trust me for a day or two with your quite remarkable find?"

"Of course, sir. To be honest, I wouldn't be able to sleep a wink if I had that on me."

"Then I'll be in touch," said Holmes, slipping the lad a few coins. "In the meantime, I would recommend avoiding the foreshore near Wapping Pier."

"Right you are, sir. And will you…?" The boy hesitated.

"Yes," answered Holmes, reading his mind. "I will most definitely see what I can do about the scoundrel who murdered poor Dickie."

"Thank you, sir!"

And with that, the boy grabbed another sandwich and exited as quickly as he had arrived. I looked up from the few notes I had managed to scribble down.

"Well?" I asked. "What do you make of it all?"

"We have enough information with which to proceed, but precisely *how* we proceed is the question. There is nothing to be done tonight, so we will attack the problem with all of the vigour at our disposal tomorrow."

When I awoke the next morning, I found Holmes already up and dressed, sitting at his desk and staring at the emerald before him. How long he had been there I had no idea, but I imagined he was running one scenario after another through his mind, calculating where the jewel might have come from, and what sort of action he might embark upon that day. There were the various issues of preserving the identity and safety of young Bisset, finding the murderer of Dickie Bentham, and solving the mystery of how and why a jewel of this splendour wound up on the banks of the Thames.

"Well, there is nothing else for it," Holmes suddenly broke his silence. "I shall have to call on Mycroft. Would you care to accompany me to Whitehall?"

Upon indicating that nothing would be give me greater pleasure than to call on Holmes's older brother, Holmes and I set sail across the city on a clear and brisk morning. Mindful of the fact that Holmes was not a man who enjoyed repeating himself, I held my tongue during our journey, quite certain that all of my questions would be answered during the conference with Mycroft.

Upon entering at Whitehall, we were swiftly and silently escorted to Mycroft Holmes's office. Aside from some well-stuffed bookshelves and a scattering of papers on the desk, there was little to indicate that it was there that the most serious business of the country was decided. From private conversations with Holmes, I had learned there was scarcely any matter of national or international importance upon which Mycroft was not consulted, and we had only waited a matter of moments before his considerable bulk navigated itself into our presence. There were no greetings or niceties exchanged between the brothers. Instead, Holmes reached into his vest pocket, removed the emerald, and held it toward Mycroft in his outstretched hand.

Taking the jewel from Holmes, Mycroft strolled to a window and held it up to the light, turning it this way and that.

"Quite a pretty little bauble," began Mycroft, "and genuine, of course. You would scarcely be here otherwise."

"Quite right," answered Holmes as Mycroft returned the stone with a shake of his head.

"There is simply no accounting for the various whims and desires of humanity," observed Mycroft. "We like to think of ourselves as being the masters of the planet, but when it comes down to it, our interests aren't any more complex or profound than those of a crow. Think of the wars that have been waged and the countless lives ruined thanks to nothing more than the lust for a shiny rock or piece of metal. We are, I'm afraid, quite a ludicrous species."

"There have been no police reports of missing jewels," remarked Holmes, "and I take it that no one in your august circles has reported such a magnificent emerald missing?"

"No," answered Mycroft, "and I would most assuredly have heard about it if Lord So-and-So or Duchess Whomever had been robbed. Personally, the whereabouts of a stone formed from hydrothermal fluids containing beryllium is of little interest to me, but as you are well aware, there is a class of people in our society to whom nothing is more important or valuable. How did the stone happen to come into your possession?"

At this, Holmes recounted the tale of Bisset almost verbatim. When he was finished, the Holmes brothers settled themselves across from one another, and what followed was a consultation that apparently required no speaking whatsoever. After some thirty seconds of this, Mycroft leaned back in his chair and drummed his fingers on the armrest.

"Not an injudicious assumption."

"So you agree?"

"No other series of circumstances fits the facts at our disposal."

"Although that possibility does exist."

"Certainly."

"Then I shall move forward with that as a working hypothesis."

"Agreed. Do keep me posted."

At this, Holmes got to his feet and Mycroft did the same. Holmes looked at the emerald in his hand. "A jewel such as this will no doubt excite a general feeling of acquisitiveness in any number of individuals, both through legal machinations and otherwise. However, it is my considered opinion that young Bisset, having risked his life to acquire it, should be the sole beneficiary of whatever monetary value it possesses. May I trust you to see to that with the expertise and discretion for which you are so justly fabled?"

A whisper of a smile crossed Mycroft's face at this gentle jibe from his younger sibling. "You may."

"Excellent. Then I shall retain the jewel for the time being, but will return it to your care at the earliest opportunity."

Exiting the building, Holmes waved down a hansom cab, and a moment later we were travelling at a brisk pace back to Baker Street. I pulled out my notebook and readied my pencil.

"'Not an injudicious assumption,'" I quoted Mycroft. "Would it be indelicate of me to ask what, precisely, that injudicious assumption might be?"

"You were there," returned Holmes. "You witnessed the climax to the entire affair. Not only that, you thought sufficiently of it to write it up as one of your tales in the somewhat lurid fashion that your readers seem to enjoy."

Now I was even more at sea than I had been previously.

"I enjoy riddles, allusions, and hints as much as the next man," I answered, my pencil hovering over my notebook, "But if you would be so kind…"

Holmes turned his gaze toward me. "Cast your mind back to the fabled Agra Treasure. The chest of priceless jewels smuggled into this country from India, and the story which was so ably recounted by you in *The Sign of the Four*. As we pursued

Jonathan Small and the Andaman Islander Tonga down the Thames, once Small despaired of making his escape – "

"He threw the Agra Treasure overboard!" I fairly shouted. "Yes, of course! And now it's those individual gems that are somehow being dredged up by the tide and deposited on the banks of the river."

"Not an injudicious assumption," answered Holmes with a smile.

"Well then, what do we do next?" I enquired. "Should we bring Scotland Yard into it?"

"I think not," answered Holmes. "While there would no doubt be some excitement at the prospect of recovering lost treasure, they would have little interest in pursuing justice on behalf little Dickie Bentham. Even if they did, that would put young Bisset in harm's way as the only witness to the crime. No, Watson, I think we shall need to expand the horizon of possibilities in this particular case, perhaps even venturing into extralegal waters."

"Then what do you propose?"

"I propose a stroll along the banks of the Thames near Wapping Pier later today, perhaps just as the sun is setting to more readily reveal whatever the tides have dredged up for a watchful observer."

"Excellent!" I agreed. "I'll bring my revolver should any of the brigands show their faces."

"Which is precisely why you will not be accompanying me on this particular expedition, Watson." Reading my confused expression, Holmes continued. "I am sincerely hoping that the brigands do show their faces."

"But Holmes," I objected, "you'll be putting yourself in harm's way!"

"To a certain extent, I suppose," agreed Holmes, "but in my profession there is bound to be a little bit of danger now and then. Hazard of the trade. All one can do is be prepared for whatever obstacles present themselves."

I was not at all pleased with Holmes's plan for the evening, but I held my tongue, well aware that a wide streak of obstinacy was a particularly salient part of his personality. As the hour of his departure neared, Holmes took the time to tidy up some of the mess he had created in our rooms, then puttered around with some sort of chemical experiment as I pondered the odds of my following Holmes without being detected. It was with some consternation, therefore, that I heard him pronounce, "The clever thing to do, of course, would be to leave before me rather than attempt to follow my footsteps. My destination is no secret, and perhaps there is some kind of structure behind which you could obscure yourself with me none the wiser."

"I am merely concerned for your safety," I returned, not bothering to try and refute Holmes's deduction.

"And your concern is duly noted and appreciated." Holmes abandoned his chemical experimentation to put on his coat and slip a revolver into his pocket. "I must confess, Watson, I'm rather excited about this expedition. I do enjoy looking for things and fancy that I have a certain facility for finding them. In this case, the possibility of turning up both a priceless gem and a murderer has my appetite rather keenly whetted. Back in a bit."

And with that, Holmes exited our rooms. I moved to our window and a moment later watched his lean form crossing Baker Street with long strides. This is what he lived for – the hunt – and I could only hope that this was not an occasion in which he would become the hunted. It was everything I could do not to follow my first instinct which, as Holmes had correctly deduced, was to shadow his footsteps, but if Holmes wished to evade me, there was little question that he could do so with ease. There was nothing for it but to wait at Baker Street and hope that he returned safely and with an interesting tale to tell.

Not surprisingly, I was more conscious of the movement of the sun than usual, and as the day waned, I pictured in my mind's eye Holmes scrambling down to the shore of the

Thames, and then picking his way amongst the debris. Even as his eagle eye scanned this way and that for anything interesting or untoward in the muck at his feet, I knew that he would also be mindful of anyone watching his movements. This ability of his, a kind of spatial awareness that allowed him to focus on the *minutiae* of a location and yet retain a bird's-eye-view, as it were, was something that I had never encountered in any of my other acquaintances. Still, my nerves were on edge as darkness fell and the minutes of the clock ticked past.

Just as I was of a mind to put on my coat and head toward Wapping Pier, I heard our downstairs door open, and a moment later a somewhat disheveled and mud-spattered Sherlock Holmes entered our rooms. His faced was flushed with excitement, and the blood from a gash above his left eye was still glistening.

"Holmes!" I cried. "You've been wounded!"

"I'm perfectly fine," he answered. "The greatest wound is to my vanity. Let me just clean up and I shall tell you all. Fetch us a brandy, will you?"

By the time Holmes emerged from his bedroom, I had stoked the fire and his brandy was waiting for him. I had already indulged in one glass and had another at my elbow as Holmes approached me, then held out his open palm.

"Not a bad evening's work, eh?"

Looking at the contents of Holmes's hand, I expected to see diamonds, a ruby or two, or perhaps a smattering of pearls. Instead, there was a Coldstream Guards button, some kind of copper badge, and a George II halfpenny which had been bent in two.

"Note the Georgian halfpenny, Watson. Young men of the period used to bend these coins to demonstrate their strength to young ladies they wished to impress. Who knows the full history behind this coin? Were I not a consulting detective, I feel quite certain that I could quite happily spend my life as an archaeologist or museum curator."

Holmes sat down and picked up his snifter of brandy.

"And your wound?" I asked. "How did you come by that?"

"Well," he answered, "I picked up my little prizes, then gave a loud shout of delight to suggest that I had found something quite valuable and remarkable. This immediately brought two antagonists into my vicinity, demanding that I come toward them and show them my treasure. I delayed, hoping to see the form of Big Jamie further up the bank, but there was no one. My new acquaintances became increasingly agitated at my hesitation, and so a brief but difficult conference ensued. One of them took to his heels almost immediately, but the other fellow remained and caught me a neat blow with a small cudgel he was carrying. I was concerned that the fellow who ran away might be summoning reinforcements, so I made arrangements to speak with my remaining assailant tomorrow."

I paused in my note-taking to look up. "Come now, Holmes. You don't mean to suggest this fellow introduced himself and handed you his card."

"Nothing quite so civilised, I'm afraid," answered Holmes as he finished his brandy and got to his feet. "But you would do me a great favour tomorrow morning if you could possibly contact some of your medical acquaintances to find a gentleman recently admitted to a hospital with a broken left fibula, a fractured orbital socket, and dislocated right thumb. Now then, if you don't mind, it has been an evening of some exertion, and I would like to rest up for tomorrow, which promises to be of an extremely stimulating nature."

I was still registering the meaning of Holmes's parting words and trying to picture the scene as I heard his bedroom door close behind him. There he had been, on the edge of the Thames, dusk gathering, as an armed assailant stood before him and one of his assailant's confederates was in the process of gathering reinforcements. Far from panicking or lashing out indiscriminately, Holmes had quite coolly calculated the very specific injuries he was about to inflict upon the man, in full knowledge that those injuries would allow him to track the man down to a hospital the next day. It was, I daresay, cold-blooded in the extreme, but only one way in which Holmes made for a far more formidable opponent than most people dreamed. He was an extremely civilised and well-mannered gentleman – up until the moment he wasn't – and not for the first time it occurred to me how happy I was to be on his side.

The next morning, as London Hospital was only a little over a mile north of Wapping Pier, I made my first enquiries there and wasn't particularly surprised to learn that a gentleman with the precise injuries described by Holmes had been admitted the previous evening. His name, or at least, the name that he gave the hospital, was William Brown. Subsequently communicating this to Holmes, we made our way to the hospital in the early afternoon, with Holmes silent and thoughtful, at one point pulling the emerald from his pocket to gaze upon it, as if all the answers to this particular case lay concealed within its deep green interior.

As we strolled the hallway of the hospital toward the infirmary, I was curious as to what information Holmes wanted to get from the man, and precisely how he would go about getting it. The beds were filled with all manner of patients with all manner of injuries or other ailments, and as he spotted us approaching, Brown's eyes went wide and he made an effort to sit up in his bed. This effort was made with some difficulty, as various bandages and plasters covered three parts of his body, and he looked every inch like a man who had been hit by a train.

"Mr. Brown, is it? I believe we made one another's acquaintance yesterday evening," said Holmes politely, only to be met by a frightened and uncomprehending stare. "No matter if you don't remember my face, but I wonder if I might have a word with you regarding your activities between Blackwall and the Plumstead Marshes, and your acquaintance with a gentleman known as Big Jamie? I am most anxious to locate him."

At this, a guttural sound of contempt emerged from the man. "I don't know nothing. Nothing. Never heard of Big Jamie."

"Ah, I fancied that might be your response," Holmes nodded, then turned to me. "Watson, I wonder if I might have a private word with Mr. Brown."

"Of course," I agreed, and with the rapid motion known to every doctor and nurse, pulled a set of curtains around the bed, leaving Holmes and the man alone. I stayed nearby, keeping an eye out for any medical personnel who might interrupt this conference and simultaneously endeavouring to hear whatever might transpire, but could make nothing out until Holmes emerged from behind the curtains less than two minutes later.

"Most illuminating," was all he said, and then I found myself trailing after his rapid stride as he made his way out of the hospital and we emerged into Whitechapel Road. As Holmes blinked into the bright afternoon sunshine, my curiosity got the better of me.

"What did he tell you?"

"Apparently, Big Jamie does consider that particular portion of the shore to be his personal stomping grounds, as it were, but last night he had overindulged in a local pub to the extent that he was unable to patrol his territory as usual. This was likely a result of him pawning whatever jewel or valuable he stole from Dickie Bentham before murdering the poor lad."

"And Mr. Brown simply volunteered this information?" I asked.

"Watson, you are a perceptive man and you have known me for some time now. In your estimation, would you say that I am a good man to cross?"

"No," I said, then added, "I should say you were the last man in London I would wish to cross."

"A conclusion that Mr. Brown apparently reached as well, with commendable alacrity, I might add." Holmes began walking and I kept by his side as he glanced at me. "Any plans for the evening?"

"No, none," I answered.

"Would you care to accompany me to the vicinity of Wapping Pier? I fancy trying my luck at a bit more mudlarking on the Thames."

"Nothing would please me more," I returned, glad that I was finally to be included more actively in this most interesting case.

By the time the sun had begun to dip toward the horizon, Holmes and I were on our way. I was pleased to see that he had armed himself, and I had my trusty Webley in my pocket as well. It is always preferable to anticipate rather than react, and if Big Jamie had somehow managed to avoid drinking himself into a stupor, I felt fairly certain that he would make an appearance before the evening was through. For some reason not quite clear to me, Holmes had brought along a bullseye lantern for the expedition, and as we neared Wapping Pier, he paused to take in our surroundings.

"I'm just going to go down over there," Holmes began, pointing to a spot some fifty yards away. "Be a good fellow and slump down against this wall like a drunken sailor, will you?"

"What?" I objected. "Let me go down with you. You have no idea what will happen. What if that murderous ruffian shows up with a gang of his men?"

"I highly doubt that. He'll have one or two assistants at the most, because he won't want to share whatever treasures are found. In fact, I'm willing to wager that Big Jamie will be entirely on his own this evening. Given that, I would prefer to have you as my reserve force, if necessary, and fancy that a single figure poking around in the mud will make a much more attractive target than two of us. Just keep an eye out and act as you see best."

And so, with some misgivings, I watched Holmes make his way to the shore while I sat myself down in the shadow of an old warehouse and kept one hand on my Webley. It was a grim spot to be sure, and it was only far up the river that I spotted any other human activity at all. The slow-flowing Thames glowed deep orange beneath the rays of the setting sun as Holmes made his way carefully across the mud, stooping every now and then to retrieve a new prize of some kind. Or was he actually retrieving anything, I wondered? Perhaps this was all a show for whatever hidden eyes might be watching him.

An enormous barge floated silently downstream as the sun finally disappeared and darkness began to gather with disconcerting rapidity. I could still see Holmes as a silhouette in the distance, and then saw the light in his bullseye lantern sending out a strong beam of illumination. This made his movements much easier to follow – not only for me, but for anyone else who might be watching him. My unease continued to increase as the minutes passed, until at length an excited cry from Holmes carried its way across the gloom. Peering into the distance, I saw him hold up the bullseye lantern, then place the emerald directly in front of the single point of light streaming from it. The gem glowed in the darkness like a green beacon and I found myself getting to my feet involuntarily.

At the same time, I became aware of a large figure disengaging itself from a tangled mass of flotsam and moving in Holmes's direction. I somehow managed to stifle the cry of warning in my throat, knowing full well that Holmes had intentionally lured his adversary into the open, but the sheer size of the man was a shock to my senses. Well over six feet tall and clearly weighing nearly thirty stone, he lumbered with surprising speed toward Holmes, yelling something indecipherable to my ears. Holmes immediately began moving away from the man, getting closer to the now black waters of the Thames as the tide began to creep back in.

This failed to deter his approaching antagonist, whose greed for the green stone he had seen in Holmes's hand had overwhelmed all his senses. Reaching into the folds of his gargantuan coat, his hand emerged holding a knife as he closed in on Holmes. No longer willing to stay in my hiding place, I rushed forward with every intention of helping Holmes fight off the giant, when the sharp retort of a pistol shot reached my ears and I saw Big Jamie stumble and then fall into the mud clutching at his leg. Holmes stood only a few feet from the man, and I could see Holmes bending down to speak to him. Whatever Holmes said, his words were met with a roar of anger followed by a torrent of abuse. A moment later the light of the bullseye lantern was bobbing in my direction, and soon Holmes had scrambled up some stairs to stand by my side, somewhat out of breath.

Like some kind of beached sea monster, the writhing figure of Big Jamie was struggling to stand up, but the thick mud of the Thames had begun to hold him fast. The tide was rushing in more rapidly now, and it was a cry of fear and terror that emerged from the giant's throat.

"Holmes," I began, "should we help him?"

"I did offer my assistance," answered Holmes, "on the condition that he confess to the murder of Dickie Bentham. You witnessed his reply."

Turning to search the pier for any associates of Big Jamie's rushing to his rescue, Holmes nodded in satisfaction as he observed that we were quite alone. Out in the darkness, Big Jamie continued to thrash helplessly in the dark muck, like a musk ox who has stumbled into a mud pit, his cries growing more feeble and hoarse as the tide continued its inexorable course toward shore and gradually engulfed him.

"He's beyond our help, Watson, and I greatly doubt that the world will mourn the passing of such a murderous ruffian," remarked Holmes as he extinguished the light in his lantern. "Let's go home. I should like to clean up."

It was several days later, as I was consolidating some notes from Holmes's previous cases, that he entered our rooms, hung up his coat, and poured himself a cup of tea.

"Would you like to hear the resolution to our little adventure near Wapping Pier?" he asked.

"I most assuredly would," I replied, turning my notebook to a blank page.

"I have just returned from a meeting with Mycroft, and you will be gratified to learn that all loose ends have been tied up."

"Mycroft's specialty," I observed.

"Indeed," answered Holmes, sipping his tea. "The body of a large but unidentifiable man was pulled from the Thames two days ago. The emerald found by young Bisset has been exchanged for a quite respectable bank account in his name at the Bank of London. At Bisset's insistence, a small portion of that money was used to purchase a headstone for Dickie Bentham. He's a good lad, Bisset. Would that more of our so-called 'respectable' fellow citizens had his sense of honour and decency. I predict a bright future for him."

"And – ?" I asked. There was one aspect of our adventure that Holmes had neglected to mention, and it was an aspect that my mind had returned to with unsettling frequency since we left Big Jamie to his fate.

"Calm yourself, Watson," answered Holmes, as he strolled to our window to look down at the hustle and bustle in Baker Street. "I don't recommend any further expeditions to Wapping Pier in search of the scattered remains of the Agra Treasure. Certainly, portions of it may wash ashore here and there over time, but I suspect that most it has already been washed to sea. Besides, as you are well aware, ravenous greed for the Agra Treasure has led more than one man to his unpleasant demise. I shouldn't like either one of us to come to a premature end in pursuit of some shiny stones."

"True," I muttered, my dreams of running my fingers through a treasure chest full of jewels dissipating rapidly.

"But don't despair," continued Holmes, leaning more closely to the window as he continued to stare out of it. "In the first place, money, as you are well aware, isn't everything. And secondly, I suspect that the recently widowed leech collector heading in our direction will present a most interesting case."

The Adventure of the
Scottish Coffins

*This tale follows the true events that began unfolding in Edin-
burgh, Scotland, in 1836, when seventeen coffins were found
hidden on the extinct volcano known as Arthur's Seat. Subsequently disappearing, eight of the coffins mysteriously reappeared in 1901, and Holmes and Watson hop aboard the Flying
Scotsman to help solve a mystery that may be related to the
murders and body-snatching activities of the notorious Burke
& Hare.*

"Coffins? In Scotland?" I found myself blinking in the morning
light streaming through my bedroom window as the indistinct
form of Sherlock Holmes stood at the foot of my bed.

"Indeed," returned Holmes. "They are awaiting our attention in Auld Reekie."

"Edinburgh?" I had managed to struggle to a seated position. "Whereabouts in Edinburgh?"

"Well, there's a bit of a story I will need to relate to you,
but they were originally found hidden on Arthur's Seat, and
since I suspect that we will be unable to convince an extinct
volcano to make its way to London, I suppose we must venture
north to investigate. Now then, if you would be so kind as to
shift yourself with a modicum of alacrity, we should be able to
catch the Flying Scotsman and have you in Edinburgh in time
for tea."

With that, Holmes disappeared, only for his head to appear
around the edge of my door frame a moment later. "No time for
breakfast, but we'll get some haggis and whisky into you once
we arrive."

Truth be told, the prospect of haggis for tea was not likely
to rouse me from my bed with anything approaching the alacrity

that Holmes had just requested, but the additional elements of a crime to be investigated and the possibility of a tasty dram or two did the trick.

Once my feet were on the floor, and having taken a moment or two to ease the stiffness out of my joints, I began rapidly assessing what I would need to have with me for this spontaneous excursion. Having experienced the vagaries of Scottish weather during my time studying medicine at the University of Edinburgh, two tweed jackets and a mackintosh were soon nestled into a travelling case, with a sturdy pair of wellies joining them a moment later. Reasoning that anything I had forgotten could be quickly procured at any of the fine establishments lining Princes Street, I soon presented myself to Holmes at the very moment Mrs. Hudson rounded a corner and regarded Holmes and me with some surprise.

"You're quite right, Mrs. Hudson," said Holmes, jumping straight into the middle of the conversation without wasting time on any preliminaries. "We are off to parts very well known. Scotland, to be precise. Your deductive faculties do you proud. Now then, during our absence, I will kindly beg you to use your Herculean powers of self-control to not enter our rooms and tidy up. I have a very delicate experiment in progress, and even the gentlest zephyr generated by the opening of the door is liable to set me back three weeks of research. Do I have your word on that?"

"Why, yes," Mrs. Hudson nodded her agreement. "Of course. Was it Scotland you said?"

"Aye, lassie." I struggled to control an outburst of mirth as Holmes continued with his version of a Scottish brogue. "It's a bonny wee land just north of here on the verge of becoming civilised. We won't be but a day or two. Come along, Doctor."

Less than a minute later, Holmes and I were seated across from one another in a cab, rattling our way across London in good time.

"Should I even ask what that was about?" I began.

Holmes offered a good-natured shrug and smiled. "Being able to speak in various languages and accents is occasionally part of my vocation. One must keep in practise."

"And was it really necessary to come up with that nonsense story about your delicate experiment?"

"I'm afraid so," Holmes leaned back and tented his fingers together. "You haven't made a study of the inner workings of Mrs. Hudson's mind as I have. Were I to simply instruct her not to enter our rooms in our absence, I guarantee you we would have returned to a scarcely recognizable scene. Books would have been reshelved, papers would have been tidied up, and so on."

"Surely not."

"For the first few hours of our absence, Mrs. Hudson would have obeyed my command to the very letter, but soon enough, chinks would have appeared in her armor of resolution. It would begin with her thinking to herself that a quick clean couldn't hurt anything. This would then progress to ruminating on my reasons for asking her not to enter our rooms. Did I, perhaps, think she was incapable of tidying up a room properly? Was this a commentary on her house-keeping skills? Was she getting on a bit and I simply didn't wish to inconvenience her? Well, that simply wouldn't do. She would show me. She would show both of us. And we would have returned to immaculate rooms wherein every surface would be polished, every wayward crumb would have been swept up, and it would have taken us a good month to return matters to our preferred conditions."

"Good God," I muttered. "That was a narrow escape then."

And as I observed the brow of Holmes shaping itself into a small furrow, I cast my glance outside at the swirling colors of early morning London, happy as always to be moving, and with a specific destination in mind. In short order, the cab delivered us to King's Cross Station, where the gently puffing Flying Scotsman seemed to be patiently waiting our arrival, as it was only moments after we boarded that I felt the lurch of the train moving forward as we settled into our seats.

With my morning fog well and truly cleared from our journey to the station, the full meaning of Holmes's rousing words came back to me in a rush. "Coffins, Holmes? Did I hear you correctly?"

"Allow me to be more precise. Seventeen coffins were originally found, but then they all mysteriously disappeared, the theory being that they had passed into the hands of private collectors."

"Private – ?" I could scarcely conceal my astonishment. "Who on earth would possibly want to collect coffins?"

Ignoring my question, Holmes continued on. "However, eight of these coffins reappeared just yesterday, and are currently awaiting our examination at the Museum of the Society of Antiquaries."

"I see," I began, trying to fashion some semblance of order out of the bizarre array of facts that Holmes had flung about in scattershot fashion. "These are relics of some kind? Coffins going back to the days of the Celtic tribes, perhaps? Were they the result of some battle or human sacrifice?"

"Not at all." Holmes's gaze was now fixed on the rapidly passing scenery outside our window. "They were originally discovered in late June of 1836. A group of young boys had taken themselves up Arthur's Seat to do some rabbit hunting, and in the manner of small boys everywhere, their enthusiasm and insatiable curiosity led them to turn over every boulder and investigate every nook and cranny that they could find. Well, they found far more than they could have ever bargained for. No fewer than seventeen coffins, carefully concealed within a cave on Arthur's Seat. As noted, they then vanished to who knows where, but now, sixty-five years later, half of them have been recovered."

"Presumably you received a communication regarding the reappearance of these coffins?" I asked. Not deigning to shift

his gaze from the window, Holmes nodded almost impercepti-
bly. "Inspector Murdoch?" I hazarded.

"The very same," answered Holmes. "Good man. It shall
be pleasant to see him again."

Now then, to provide my readers with some context for a
case to which I have never referred, Holmes was speaking of
events that had taken place four years previously, also in Edinburgh, but an urgent medical matter had precluded my accompanying Holmes. It was either an unfortunate accident or a nasty
bit of business involving an enterprising gentleman by the name
of Alf Smith, who had made a fortune for himself by contriving
a new acid formula to aid in the tanning of leather, and had built
himself a factory on the banks of the River Mersey in Manches-
ter. His labour practises and policy of dumping used chemicals
directly into the river had not endeared him to the local inhabitants, so he used a portion of his fortune to buy himself a large
estate and ruined medieval castle outside of Edinburgh, and
upon his visits to the city, had begun styling himself as Laird
Dalhousie. This had been irritating enough for the local inhabitants, but their ire steadily grew as the self-minted Laird began
appearing in public in full Scottish regalia, from his kilt right
down to his sporran, with a *sgian-dubh* tucked inside one of his
socks. When visiting pubs and engaging the locals in various
spirited discussions, he had the habit of pulling out this small
dagger and driving it into the table for emphasis.

Increasingly exasperated at the lack of respect he felt that
his newly acquired real estate should bring him, the breaking
point came on a rainy evening at Deacon Brodie's Tavern. In
the midst of a heated political argument, to the astonishment of
everyone present, Alf Smith, the born and bred Mancunian, had
begun speaking with a thick Scottish brogue. Accounts from
this point on differ, but they agree that various chairs and stools
had been raised over various heads, and that Laird Dalhousie
had fled outside into the teeming downpour. In his panic, he ran

in the direction of Arthur's Seat, with several of the more incensed tavern patrons in hot pursuit. In the end, Alf Smith, the erstwhile Laird Dalhousie, had never been seen alive again. His body was recovered from some tangled brush on the steep slopes of Arthur's Seat the next morning, and on the basis of his title alone, local officials had encouraged Inspector Murdoch to call in an outside authority, who arrived in the person of Sherlock Holmes.

The coroner's report revealed no wounds upon Laird Dalhousie's body, and concluded that he had died of exposure as the cold rain had continued to fall during the night. Had he been chased or pushed off the edge of the path? The steady rain had thoroughly effaced any and all footprints that might have assisted Holmes in his enquiry, and to a man, the patrons of Deacon Brodie's Pub had quite cheerfully provided alibis for one another. The most striking thing about the case from my perspective was that, upon his return to London, Holmes had described Inspector Murdoch as a gentleman who was "observant, diligent, and keeps his own counsel." This alone put him streets ahead of the police personnel typically encountered by Holmes, and as the Flying Scotsman sped its way north, I found myself quite looking forward to meeting this exemplar of his profession.

In the meantime, my stomach let loose a low growl to express its unhappiness with being empty, and I saw Holmes smiling across at me.

"I do apologize for rushing you off like this and disturbing your morning routine, Watson. Particularly your need to feed at regular intervals."

Was that a glint of amusement I saw in Holmes's eye? If it was, then I was perfectly prepared to amuse myself at his expense in return.

"No bother at all," I assured him. "I'll just take myself off to the dining car and see what they have."

Rising from my seat, I was gratified to see the faintest expression of bewilderment cross Holmes's face, and almost in spite of himself he uttered, "Dining car?"

"Part of the recently completed modernisation on the Flying Scotsman," I explained. "Not only did they add corridors between the cars, but they also installed heating and added dining cars. I do like to keep up on our advances in transportation. Eminently civilised, wouldn't you agree?"

"Quite," nodded Holmes. "Come to think of it, I wouldn't mind a spot of tea myself."

"Well then, join me," I said as I slid open the door to our compartment, and a moment later Holmes and I were strolling through the swaying carriage towards the nearest dining car. As we sat down and were presented with menus, Holmes surveyed our surroundings and fellow passengers, giving a nod of approval.

"Very nice," he began. "The last time I took this train, there was a half-hour stopover in York for lunch, which I thought was a ridiculous waste of time. This is, as you say, much more civilised."

I nodded, my attention more fixated on the menu than Holmes's approbation, and twenty minutes later, as I delved into my second quite acceptable soft-boiled egg, Holmes turned his attention from the window and enquired, "Did you ever have the pleasure of ascending Arthur's Seat during your university days?"

"No," I answered. "I wasn't in Edinburgh to go hill-climbing, I was there to study medicine. I did know several fellows who enjoyed taking the local girls up there. Apparently, the uneven walking paths afforded many opportunities to offer a steadying arm or hand."

"And presumably the young maidens saw to it that they were suitably unsteady."

Not for the first time, Holmes's cynicism regarding the world of courting and romance raised its head and, not for the first time, it led me to wonder where the roots of his dismissive and contemptuous feelings for the softer emotions lay. Past experience allowed me to say with absolute certainty that any enquiries along those lines would be utterly fruitless, so I spread a good dollop of Robertson's Golden Shred Marmalade on my toast and allowed my gaze to wander to the passing scenery.

We passed the next minute or two in silence, but I was well aware that Holmes's mind was spinning at its usual rate, and I took it upon myself to see if I could somehow deduce his current train of thought. He had just mentioned Arthur's Seat. Therefore, it made perfect sense that he was still musing upon that topic, so with another eight hours ahead of us on the train, I saw no harm in hazarding a guess.

"I quite agree," I announced.

Holmes looked at me in surprise. "What's that?"

"The fact that the Scottish Lowlands are home to an extinct volcano is quite remarkable. Very remarkable, indeed."

"Ah, yes," Holmes nodded. "The etymology of the name, Arthur's Seat, is obscure, but geologists estimate its age to be greater than one-hundred-million years old. It provides excellent panoramic views of the city of Edinburgh and surrounding countryside, and was described by native son Robert Louis Stevenson as, '*a hill for magnitude, a mountain in virtue of its bold design.*'"

I smiled at Holmes, more than a trifle pleased with myself, "I fancied that's what you were thinking about."

"When?"

"Just now."

"Oh, I see. Actually, I'm afraid my thoughts had strayed into criminal realms – specifically, crimes associated with the city of Edinburgh."

"Any crime in particular?" I asked.

"Burke and Hare, of course," answered Holmes. "Surely you would agree that the murderous careers of those two bold entrepreneurs rank among the very worst atrocities ever committed in these Isles. Also quite instructive when considering human behavior in its more extreme manifestations."

"In what way?" Dabbing at the corners of my mouth with a white linen napkin, I took another sip of tea and leaned back in my chair. "I can't say I'm overly familiar with their crimes, aside from the fact that they were as sensational as they were horrible."

"Then allow me to fill you in. It will enable you to be a more active participant in our investigation." Holmes produced a pipe from one of his pockets, along with a pouch of tobacco. A few moments later, a gentle puff of smoke made its way towards the ceiling of the dining car, and Holmes proceeded to embark on a tale of intrigue and murder.

"The events took place in 1828, and were a direct result of the needs of one Dr. Robert Knox, a Scottish anatomist and ethnologist whose career ended in disgrace. He was, by all accounts, an extremely intelligent yet extraordinary unpleasant individual, perhaps due to a severe bout of smallpox as a child, which had left him severely disfigured. After graduating from the University of Edinburgh, he toured the world as a physician for hire, but eventually returned to Edinburgh, where he joined an anatomy school in Surgeon's Square in 1825.

"Now then, prior to the Anatomy Act of 1832, anatomists and their students were forced to rely solely on the bodies of criminals who had been condemned to death and dissection by the courts. These weren't in abundance, and the so-called 'French Method' of teaching anatomy required one body per student, so to make up for the shortfall in corpses, the practise of grave-robbing grew in popularity. After the death of a loved one, families would have to set up a vigil near the grave to prevent it from being violated, and it is here that one William Hare enters the picture.

"There is no record of him being accused of grave-robbing, but in late 1827, an indebted lodger passed away under his roof, and Hare subsequently sold the body to Knox, who by that time had amassed more private students than any other physician in the city. This event apparently set the wheels turning in Hare's mind, and after consulting with his friend William Burke, they joined forces to begin murdering poor people in the city's Old Town and delivering the bodies to Knox, whose dissection theatre was described as a 'charnel house.' Known as the West Port Murders, Burke and Hare collected eight to ten pounds per body, which was quite a tidy sum of money to be spent on all the delights that Edinburgh had to offer, up until the day they were both arrested. Questions?"

The abruptness of Holmes's query caught me off guard, and it took me a moment to collect my thoughts and ask, "Presumably both scoundrels were hanged?"

"Not at all," answered Holmes. "The case against them was actually quite weak, and it was only when Hare turned King's Evidence that Burke was convicted and hanged in front of a crowd estimated to be at least twenty-five thousand people. Appropriately enough, he was then publicly dissected at the University of Edinburgh's Old College. His skeleton was given to the Anatomical Museum of the Edinburgh Medical School, and reputedly a pocket book was bound with his tanned skin, an unusual but by no means unique practice known as *anthropodermic bibliopegy*. It's currently on display at the Surgeons' Hall Museum. I'm must confess that I'm disappointed to learn that you aren't aware of these admittedly insalubrious details."

"I was in Edinburgh to learn the art of medicine!" I replied somewhat heatedly. "Not to gawk at some macabre souvenirs! And what about William Hare then? He was the instigator of the entire affair. Was his skull made into a chalice and his bones into some kind of musical instrument?"

"Better than that, Watson," answered Holmes. "Much better than that. No one knows."

"No one knows what?"

"What happened to William Hare. He was promised immunity to provide testimony against his former partner, and he was last seen heading south towards England. His ultimate fate remains unknown to this day."

This put me back on my heels, as it were. Was this the purpose of Holmes's desire to visit Edinburgh? To somehow pick up the trail of William Hare and determine his eventual fate? But no. We were heading north to view some coffins. Holmes had said as much. How had the conversation veered into this unpleasant direction? Before I could begin to assemble my thoughts to ask further questions, Holmes interrupted me.

"There is one more feature to the Burke and Hare case of which you should be aware – that is, their number of victims."

"It was…" I began to rack my memory, but with no success. "I can't remember the precise number, but it was not insubstantial."

"Sixteen."

I stared at Holmes. Now it was all coming together in a rush. Seventeen coffins found on Arthur's Seat and sixteen victims of Burke and Hare. They couldn't possibly be connected, could they?

"The number may be slightly fewer or slightly more," added Holmes. "Burke and Hare proved to be peculiarly reticent when it came to providing precise figures, as was Dr. Knox."

"Whatever happened to this Knox fellow?" I asked.

"He was never prosecuted," said Holmes, "arguing that he was entirely unaware of the murderous activities of Burke and Hare. He was merely the happy recipient of the extremely fresh corpses they provided. However, his dark reputation in Edinburgh made life difficult for him, so he subsequently removed himself to London where he wrote two popular books: one on salmon fishing in Scotland, and the other on ethnology and race. He was particularly keen on the idea that Irish Catholics should be utterly eradicated from the face of the earth for the benefit of humanity."

Holmes paused as he took in my shocked expression. "And that, my dear Watson, is why human beings will remain a never-ending subject of study, speculation, and grief to one another."

By the time we arrived at Edinburgh's Waverley Station, I had decided to give up on making any sense of this mad journey, and allow Holmes and time to reveal what they would reveal. As various disembarking passengers hurried to meet friends and relatives, I spied a small, unmoving figure at the back of the platform, and somehow conceived the idea that this must be none other than Inspector Murdoch as I had pictured him in my mind. To my pleasant surprise, I was proved correct, as Holmes grasped my elbow and led me towards this paragon of Scottish policemen.

"Inspector Murdoch," began Holmes, "this is my friend and colleague, Dr. Watson, without whom I would be utterly lost. Watson, this is the estimable Murdoch."

He couldn't have been much over five feet tall and weighed no more than ten stone, but his crystal blue eyes held mine unwaveringly as he shook my hand and I felt the rough skin of a man who had been raised doing more than his fair share of manual labour.

"Coffins or hotel?" asked Murdoch in a soft Scottish brogue.

"Coffins, of course," answered Holmes. "As you can see, we haven't much baggage and can carry what we have with us."

As we settled into the carriage provided by Murdoch, Holmes looked at the small figure sitting across from him with a smile. "Now then, I would imagine that it isn't every day that eight coffins magically appear on your doorstep."

"No indeed," answered Murdoch. "And it was scarcely a minute later that I composed a telegram to be sent to you. I felt quite certain you would find the news, shall we say, of interest."

"And here I am," answered Holmes.

"Here you are," repeated Murdoch.

"You have your opinion," ventured Holmes.

"I do," replied Murdoch, "but should be glad of yours."

"And you shall have it."

The two men nodded at one another, and the remainder of our journey was passed in silence until we pulled up outside the Museum of the Society of Antiquaries. As we approached the entrance, I observed the Coat of Arms of the society emblazoned with the St. Andrews Cross near the top of an archway. It was clear that our arrival was expected, as one doorway after another was opened for us, until we arrived at a small room at the end of a long corridor.

It was Murdoch himself who produced a key and pronounced, "The coffins of Arthur's Seat, gentlemen." With that, he opened the door and ushered us into a space not larger than a small bedroom. There would scarcely have been room for eight coffins, and as I looked around, I discerned none at all. The day had begun with some degree of discombobulation, and as I stood there looking around in bewilderment, I began to suspect that this was nothing more than some grand joke concocted by Holmes with the assistance of his friend Inspector Murdoch. Just as I was on the verge of expressing my exasperation and outrage, Murdoch lifted a cloth from a small table, and as he whisked it away, I observed to my astonishment eight miniature coffins. Each one could not have been more than four inches in length and perhaps an inch or two across. In an instant, Holmes had brought out his magnifying lens and was examining the exteriors of the coffins with the utmost concentration. Small, involuntary sounds began to emerge from Holmes, and as I glanced at Murdoch, I saw a small smile on his face.

When Holmes removed the lids from the coffins, my astonishment grew, for inside each coffin was a small figure. Each of these figures was examined in turn by Holmes with painstaking attention to the figures themselves, as well as to the various styles of clothing that had been glued and stitched onto them. This analysis went on for several minutes, at which point, without a word, Holmes turned and handed his magnifying lens to me. I dutifully bent over to conduct my own examination of the coffins and figures, all the while highly conscious of the fact that the odds of me perceiving anything that had escaped Holmes's attention were very slim indeed. However, the fact that Holmes had been kind enough include me in his investigation filled me with pride, and I was especially pleased that this small gesture would elevate me in the estimation of Inspector Murdoch as well.

To my eye, the dolls all seemed to be representations of adults, with roughly carved features that didn't betray the hand of an especially skilled artisan. Some of the figures were without arms, presumably for the simple reason that they wouldn't have fit into the coffins otherwise. I observed what appeared to be spectacles drawn onto one or two of the faces, but beyond that failed to discern anything particularly remarkable. After what seemed to me to be a suitable amount of time for a thorough investigation, I handed Holmes his magnifying lens. Rather than launch into a lengthy disquisition of my thoughts, I reasoned that given the situation and the company, this might be a good time to keep things brief.

"Fascinating," I offered.

"Indeed," confirmed Holmes. "If you might give us a chance to change into more suitable clothing, Murdoch, I would like to see where these coffins were found originally."

"Of course," answered Murdoch. "I arranged for accommodations at The George Hotel. I trust that will meet your needs."

"Excellent," replied Holmes. "Then Watson and I will join you at Arthur's Seat in one hour."

By the time we reached our hotel, a fine, misting rain had begun to settle on the city, and so it was that when we joined Inspector Murdoch at the foot of Arthur's Seat, I was fully clad in my mackintosh and wellies for the trek ahead. It wasn't a particularly arduous climb, for Arthur's Seat presents the hiker with gentle slopes swathed in brilliant green, and walking paths have been worn into the side of the hill thanks to the countless travellers over the centuries who have been lured by humanity's seemingly innate urge to climb to the top of the highest peak in the vicinity.

We were only ten minutes into our ascent when Holmes and Murdoch paused to look over a precipice that plunged down into a sea of heather and brambles. I immediately assumed that this was the spot where the late Laird Dalhousie had met his fate, an assumption that Holmes quickly verified as he turned to Murdoch.

"No further news on what happened to his Lairdship?" he asked.

"None," answered Murdoch. "As far as the locals were concerned, it was as if nothing at all had transpired, although I will say that more than the usual number of toasts were offered in the city's pubs."

Murdoch picked up a sizable stone, glistening from the rain, and with a gentle motion tossed it down into the chasm of foliage beneath us. It rustled a few leaves before it was swallowed up, presumably to remain untouched by human hands for the next few centuries.

"It's a natural thing for our arrival into this world to be celebrated," mused Murdoch, "but when your departure is celebrated even more, it's fair to say that your time on earth was not well spent."

With that, Murdoch resumed his upward climb, Holmes and I following him, until we rounded a corner and Murdoch led us to a cleft in the rock that opened up into a very small cave.

"Originally," began Murdoch, "this cave was hidden behind three slabs of slate that the boys were able to move to gain access. And it was here they found seventeen wee coffins. They were arranged in three tiers, two tiers of eight, and then a single coffin placed on top."

Holmes inspected the cramped space closely, then ventured back outside the cave to get his bearings.

"Northeast side of the hill," he began, "the pieces of slate not only protecting the coffins from the elements, but also from prying eyes. Were it not for the curious boys, they could have remained here undetected for decades, if not centuries."

"Shall we retire to Deacon Brodie's for a pint or two to discuss the matter?" asked Murdoch.

"Capital!" replied Holmes, and as he glanced at me, I nodded my enthusiastic agreement, especially at the prospect of a pint accompanied by a meat pie or an old favorite from my university days, bangers and mash.

The tavern was only half-full when we entered, and as my eyes adjusted to the dimness, I became aware that everyone in attendance had turned our way as we sat down at a corner table near the fire. The presence of Murdoch appeared to assure the locals that Holmes and I weren't strangers looking for trouble, and it seemed we had barely sat down and divested ourselves of our damp garments when three pints of bitter appeared, followed by an assortment of meat and pork bridies. There then followed several minutes of silence as we turned our attention to the food and drink, but at length Murdoch pushed his chair back an inch or two with a satisfied sigh and glanced at Holmes, who was in the process of lighting his pipe.

"I will take it for granted," began Murdoch, "that you have already formulated your own theories, so I will offer you my impressions and see to what extent they coincide with your own."

"That will be fine, Murdoch," answered Holmes. "I was hoping for as much."

"Then let us start with the Lilliputian coffins themselves," said Murdoch. "At one point in time, they weren't in existence, yet some event or series of events, prompted an unknown individual to create them. I say 'individual' because I feel certain that they were the product of a single hand. There is a marked similarity between all of the coffins, and while the figures inside them vary, I note the same carving marks, presumably made by the same carving tools. What sort of tools were they, and what sort of person would have had access to those particular tools? Taking together the iron embellishments, the type of nails used, and the carving marks made by a sharp, hooked knife, they are all consistent with the implements typically used by a cordwainer."

"Or perhaps a cobbler," added Holmes. "And to my eye, all of the coffins appear to have been carved from the same piece of wood."

"Agreed," said Murdoch, "which indicates they were likely manufactured at approximately the same time."

"Does the upright bearing, flat feet, and swinging arms of the figures suggest anything to you?" asked Holmes.

"It would support the idea of toy soldiers," answered Murdoch, "save for the variations in attire or costumes. Recall, if you will, the figure with the high starched collar and matching coat and pants with blue stripes. Before your arrival, I did take the liberty of consulting a local haberdasher whose family have lived here for the past two centuries. He was able to confirm that the styles of clothing on the dolls were consistent with the late 1820s and early 1830s."

"Excellent work," nodded Holmes. "So then, let us turn to the rationale behind the creation of the dolls. They were not an inconsiderable amount of labour, so why create them only to hide them away?"

"There is the possibility of some association with witchcraft and demonology," offered Murdoch, "the idea being to entomb the likenesses of people the creator wished to destroy."

"In ancient Saxony," added Holmes, "there was a tradition of burying effigies of departed loved ones who had died in distant lands."

"There is also a superstition among some sailors," continued Murdoch, "in which they ask their families or wives to give a proper Christian burial to an effigy of them should they be lost at sea."

"Which brings to mind the old German seafaring tradition, in which small dolls or mandrake roots were the kind of talismans kept in small coffins and sold as lucky charms to sailors about to start a voyage," said Holmes.

A moment of silence fell over the table, and it was then that Holmes turned to me. "Watson? You have seen everything that Inspector Murdoch and I have seen. Have you developed any theories?"

As pleased as I was to be included in the discussion, I wasn't prepared to offer any answer that I felt would provide a definitive solution to the mystery. Still, I was among friends, and aided and abetted by the courage of two pints, I spoke my mind.

"There is the old saying that for a carpenter every problem is a nail and every solution is a hammer. As detectives, you're both drawn to, shall we say, somewhat dark conclusions when presented with a mystery. But perhaps there is nothing evil or nefarious about these figures at all. Besides their bizarre appearance and the fact that they were hidden in an extinct volcano, let's not lose sight of what they are: *Dolls*. Dolls are for children, yes? Perhaps some shoemaker put them together for a young child as a present, then didn't want to risk having them found in the house, so he hid them on Arthur's Seat, but then some tragedy befell him, so there they sat until they were discovered."

As I inwardly braced for some kind of dismissive comment from either Murdoch or Holmes, instead another silence fell upon the table, before Murdoch examined the dregs of his glass and declared, "That is a possibility. Or perhaps the dolls were simply part of some macabre practical joke, the best of which unfold when the perpetrator is nowhere near the scene. But what about you, Mr. Holmes? You've heard the theories of Dr. Watson and myself. Have you one of your own?"

"I do," said Holmes, sending a puff of smoke towards the ceiling. "My theory is one of context. That is, one that depends

150

on the series of events that would have led to the creation of the dolls. I fear it isn't a theory that I will ever be able to prove, but I feel quite certain that the manufacturing of the dolls and their subsequent placement on Arthur's Seat was the work of none other than William Hare."

At this, Murdoch and I exchanged a glance as Holmes took another puff on his pipe, then leaned back in his chair and fixed his gaze upon the ceiling.

"Do go on, Mr. Holmes," said Murdoch.

"As Watson will tell you, my interest in crime and sensational literature is longstanding, and the crimes of Burke and Hare have always exerted a certain fascination. William Hare and William Burke were both Irishmen who wound up in Edinburgh and formed a friendship, no doubt based in part on their common backgrounds. Hare and his wife or partner ran a lodging house in Tanner's Close and, when a lodger died owing rent, it was only natural that Hare would bemoan this loss of income to his friend Burke. They soon landed upon the happy idea of selling the lodger's corpse to Dr. Robert Knox for a tidy sum, where they were informed that fresh corpses were always welcome.

"Following this, I would argue that Burke took the lead in this partnership. While they often teamed up to end the lives of other unfortunate lodgers, in his confession, Burke noted several occasions where he was the sole perpetrator. He had no qualms about killing and he was quite adept at it. He took a special pleasure in suffocating intoxicated women. As the old rhyme describing the roles of Burke, Hare, and Knox went:

> *Up the close and doon the stair,*
> *But and ben wi' Burke and Hare*
> *Burke's the butcher, Hare's the thief*
> *Knox the boy that buys the beef.*

"As I related to Watson on our journey here, with the promise of immunity dangled before him, it was Hare who testified against his old partner, and Burke was subsequently hanged, with Hare reputedly making his way to England, where he no doubt changed his name and disappeared from the historical records. And I would wager that it was during this period, as he strove to keep his anonymity, that the enormity of his crimes began to weigh on his conscience. No fewer than sixteen people hadn't only been murdered, but then denied a proper Christian burial as they were dissected into pieces by Knox. And so, William Hare began to roughly carve the figures we have seen with his unpractised hand. He clothed them, enclosed them in rough-hewn coffins, and then made his way back to Edinburgh, no doubt in some kind of disguise. He couldn't risk being seen in the city proper or being caught digging small graves in a cemetery, so he made his way up Arthur's Seat, found a suitable cave protected from the elements, and deposited the coffins there."

"But Holmes," I objected, "there were *seventeen* coffins, and only *sixteen* victims."

"Two rows of eight, Watson," answered Holmes, "with a single coffin placed atop them. The sixteen coffins represented the victims of Burke and Hare. The single coffin, of course, would be for his erstwhile partner, William Burke, whom he betrayed to the hangman's noose and then the anatomist's dissection table."

At this, Murdoch and I looked to one another, then back at Holmes, marvelling at the tale he had just told. It was a long and convoluted chain to be sure, but every link rang true.

"Merely a theory," added Holmes, "and we will never be able to verify whether it is true or not. Still, it has been a pleasant adventure nevertheless. Perhaps a dram or two of whisky to round off our day, gentlemen?"

This most excellent suggestion was immediately acceded to, and it was some time later that we said our good-byes to Inspector Murdoch and made our way to The George Hotel, where a soft bed and dreamless night awaited.

The next morning found neither Holmes nor myself particularly interested in conversation, and we arrived at the Waverley platform for our return journey aboard the Flying Scotsman in relative silence. Once settled into our seats, I observed Holmes's heavy lids drooping, and I must have dozed off myself, for it was a full three hours later that I awakened to find us speeding through the English countryside on our way back to London. Holmes had recovered somewhat as well, as he had procured a newspaper and was absorbed in an article of some kind. Waiting until he turned the page, I asked the question that had occurred to me the previous evening, and now seemed to demand an answer.

"Why, Holmes?"

As Holmes dipped his newspaper, I saw that his grey eyes had resumed their typical alertness. "What's that?"

"Why did we travel to Edinburgh? There was no crime to investigate, and even if you had somehow managed to forge a definite connection between those dolls and Burke and Hare, the crimes and the people who committed them are ancient history. So why make the journey at all?"

Holmes thoughtfully folded up his newspaper and regarded me with a steady gaze. "Not an injudicious question, Watson, so one that I will attempt to answer fully. First, I would draw your attention to the value of movement for its own sake. Mind and body tend to stagnate if we stay in one place for too long. In the case of London, it is a city that is quite refreshing to leave, and then there is the added benefit that one sees it more clearly, in all its splendour and squalor, upon returning.

"Then there is the always edifying practise of studying crime in all of its manifestations. So then, let us divide criminal activities into two categories: crimes of passion and crimes of profit. Invariably, crimes of passion are more easily solved because no planning or foresight has gone into them. They occur in the heat of the moment and the perpetrator is invariably apprehended quite quickly. Contrast this to crimes of profit, where the planning may be rudimentary or extremely complex, but these crimes are committed with some degree of mindfulness in the hope of not being caught or punished in any way. They are typically committed by men who focus almost exclusively on what benefits them, and they are unmindful or disinterested in how their actions might affect other people. For them, there really is no concern regarding what is right and what is wrong. It is simply a matter of what they can get away with.

"It is these depraved individuals who are the implacable enemies of every society within which they exist. Men not dissimilar to you and me in appearance, but oceans away from us in terms of values and common decency. They are predators, and their prey is their fellow human beings. This tendency is clearly exemplified in the activities of Burke and Hare. They bore no malice towards their victims. Theirs was a business enterprise, nothing less and nothing more. Indeed, in terms of business philosophy, their practices weren't dissimilar to the practices of the late Laird Dalhousie."

"Come now, Holmes!" I expostulated. "You can't compare the two. Burke and Hare were murderers and Laird Dalhousie was a businessman."

"A businessman quite content to poison his own community to increase his profits," answered Holmes. "Happy to use child labour and equally happy to pour the toxic dregs of his factory into the River Mersey, with not a single care how those corrosive chemicals might affect the communities downstream. Beware of esteemed industrialists and captains of industry, Watson. All too often, forests, rivers, and other human beings are simply commodities to be used up in their view of the world. As the French novelist Balzac expressed it: '*Behind every great fortune lies a great crime.*' And as the twentieth century gathers steam, you can be certain that technology and industrialization will enable unscrupulous men to further indulge their darkest urges, even at the risk of eradicating humanity itself. That is why it's important to understand where that criminal impulse arises, how it grows, and to what it can lead. To turn a blind eye to the activities of these men is to condemn our own species to oblivion. You may count on that."

"That's a terribly grim prognostication, Holmes," I said.

"Indeed. But picture men like Burke and Hare as the heads of government and industry, in charge of increasingly powerful machines and weaponry, and I fear that the future is bleak. In the meantime, we do what we can, old friend."

Holmes turned his gaze to the passing scenery and I observed an almost wistful expression upon his face. When he spoke again it was in an almost inaudible whisper.

"We do what we can."

Murder in Grasmere

The beautiful village of Grasmere, set in the Lake District of England, is best-known for its association with poets such as William Wordsworth and Samuel Taylor Coleridge, as well as the legendary Grasmere Gingerbread Shop. When a bizarre murder disturbs the sanctity of this bucolic setting, who better to travel north from London and solve it than Sherlock Holmes and Dr. Watson? And if, perhaps, the murder purifies the air a bit in this cozy little corner of the country, just how motivated will Holmes be to identify the murderer?

I suppose, by exercising my imagination to its utmost, that I could conjure up a more unpleasant way to start the day. Perhaps a roaring conflagration sweeping down Baker Street in such a fashion as to put the Great Fire of London in 1666 to shame. Perhaps the cries of newsboys heralding a Mongol Invasion on the south coast of England. Still, being summoned to the bedside of Muriel Higgins at an ungodly hour of the morning by her doting husband was bad enough. When I opened the door to see the bald head and squinting green eyes of Mortimer Higgins, not a word needed to be exchanged between us. I immediately fetched my trusty black medical bag and dutifully followed him three blocks down the street to attend to the spectacularly hypochondriacal Mrs. Higgins and pull her once again from death's door.

In the past year, she had contrived, in her own mind, to contract not only bubonic plague and dengue fever, but also gout, diphtheria, and tuberculosis. Fortunately, my soothing bedside manner and the occasional administration of headache powder had inspired a brisk recovery on all of these occasions. I had long since given up any hope of convincing her that her various ailments existed almost entirely in her own mind, because I finally realized the root cause behind all of her assorted crises.

Her episodes, bouts, and bad turns were all simply a way of giving her patient husband reasons to dote on her more than he already did. He would stand patiently at the foot of the bed, a small smile on his face, as I examined the invalid from head to foot, and invariably prescribed a strong cup of tea and a nice walk in the park. They were an odd pair to be sure, but they had settled on the kind of marriage that suited them both, and that was that.

My mood was by no means improved when I emerged from their flat to find that it had begun to rain, although not in earnest. Eschewing the possibility of hailing a hansom cab, I simply quickened my step and soon found myself slightly out of breath as I ascended the seventeen steps to our rooms. By this point, my friend Sherlock Holmes was already up and staring out our window onto Baker Street with a pensive expression on his face. He didn't bother to acknowledge my arrival in the slightest, not when I took a few moments to put on some dry clothes, not when Mrs. Hudson kindly brought in a pot of fresh tea, and not when I ventured to the window myself to see what he might be looking at. It was only when I had made myself comfortable in my armchair that he deigned to speak, laconically remarking, "May I take it that you have once again heroically rescued Mrs. Higgins from death's door?"

"You may," I returned, but I was still in such a peevish state of mind that I couldn't be bothered to ask Holmes how he had managed to come to that quite accurate conclusion with not a word from me.

Still, without even a glance in my direction, Holmes continued, "Mr. Higgins is possessed of a rather distinctive knocking style—three normal taps followed by two more solid blows to our door. I then watched as you returned on foot to our rooms, so your excursion was short enough to not require a cab. You were slightly damp as you came in, but not drenched through, which confirmed that your walk was a short one, and the presence of your medical bag indicated you had been called out on professional duties."

"Bravo," I muttered, and it was only then that Holmes turned from the window.

"Oh dear," he said. "I fear that I have begun to bore my dutiful chronicler with my rather tiresome deductive observations. I'm merely keeping in practice, dear fellow."

"For what?" I answered. "We haven't had an interesting case in the past two months."

This elicited an amused chuckle from Holmes. "My word. The good doctor is most definitely out of sorts on this damp summer day. Perhaps this might change your mood."

With that, Holmes dropped a telegram into my lap, and I picked it up to read:

MURDER MOST FOUL IN GRASMERE. LEPIDOP-
TERIST DEAD. PLEASE COME IF POSSIBLE.
--WILLADSEN

"Grasmere?" I looked up at Holmes. "That's in the Lake District."

"Geographically correct," he answered.

"And a lepidopterist is someone who studies and collects butterflies."

"Watson, your early morning house-call has honed your wits to a razor's edge."

At this, I felt what little energy I had ebb out of me. Mrs. Higgins had started the job, and now Holmes's sarcastic remark had finished it. I couldn't expect an apology from Holmes, but recognizing that he had gone a bit too far, Holmes proceeded to tap me gently on the shoulder, then topped off my cup of tea. Raising it to my lips, I decided to give Holmes one more chance to offer something more than a clipped and unhelpful reply.

"Do you know this Willadsen?"

"I do," answered Holmes. "Alan Willadsen. Quite an amiable young chap who cut his policing teeth with six months as a London constable, but who fancied himself as a poet more than anything else. When the opportunity arose to take a position in Grasmere, he was off like a shot, no doubt hoping that the salutary atmosphere which inspired both Wordsworth and Coleridge would guide his pen as well. He's been up there nearly two years now, and for all I know this may be the first crime he has encountered in that famously pastoral setting."

"So then, are you going to Grasmere?" I asked.

"I don't see why not," said Holmes. "I have a consultation with my brother Mycroft tomorrow evening regarding a delicate situation unfolding in Amsterdam, but in the meantime a brief trip north would not be amiss. The train from Euston Station departs for Oxenholme in the Lake District in one hour. We'll have to switch trains to make our way to Windermere, after which it will have to be a cab to Grasmere."

"'We'll?'" I had snatched at the only word I had really heard.

"If I might have the pleasure of your company," said Holmes. "Mind you, if Mrs. Higgins looks likely to take a turn for the worse, I'll understand perfectly if you prefer to stay in London."

I only heard those last few words dimly, as I had already made my way to my bedroom to pack quickly for the adventure ahead. Grasmere! I had heard the name, of course, but had never had the privilege of visiting there in person. It was a small enough village, but its reputation as a hub of literary activity in the early part of the nineteenth century put it on a par with any other city in England, save London itself. There was no time for me to do a quick review of the Lake District and its various celebrated inhabitants, but a long train ride with Holmes would doubtless leave me a veritable fount of information in the next few hours. Truth be told, Holmes and I made an excellent pair in this regard. He enjoyed regaling me with examples of his admittedly prodigious knowledge, and I marvelled at all of the events and personalities of which I had only the most perfunctory knowledge.

It was only as we settled into our seats as the train puffed away quietly in Euston Station, that I began to have some misgivings regarding just how informed Holmes might be on the literary giants associated with the Lake District. They were, after all, poets, and poetry was not a topic likely to play a significant role in the life of a consulting detective. On the other hand, he was Holmes, and it appeared to me on more than one occasion that he had somehow assembled his vast warehouse of knowledge almost by osmosis. Merely put him in a room with *The Twelve Caesars* by Suetonius and an hour later he would be able to write a treatise on the life of the Emperor Tiberius. This was patently ridiculous, of course, but Holmes's offhand remarks on subjects as diverse as the religious practices of the Aztecs and the life cycle of the duck-billed platypus had amazed me upon more than one occasion.

It was only as the train began to pick up speed on its way out of London that I looked across at Holmes with raised eyebrows and he instantly took my meaning, shaking his head in response.

"I'm afraid that my knowledge of the Lake District and its famous poets is rudimentary at best. I was rather hoping you might fill me in, old fellow. You are the writer, after all."

"Writer, yes," I replied, a feeling of disappointment settling over me. "Poet, no. I'm afraid it's a literary form that never quite caught my fancy."

"Ah, well," Holmes turned his gaze out the window. "I do know that Thomas De Quincey was a frequent visitor to Grasmere. Perhaps we can take some inspiration from him."

"What?" I answered, a faint feeling of alarm running through me. "The author of *Confessions of an English Opium-Eater*? Surely not."

"No, no, nothing of the kind." Holmes pulled out his pipe and began to tamp it down. "Some years after overcoming his laudanum addiction, De Quincey published a trilogy of essays whose subject matter is much more in line with my own interests—'On Murder Considered as one of the Fine Arts.' Let us hope that the crime Willadsen has for us is of some interest, perhaps even venturing into the artistic realms so enthusiastically described by De Quincey."

"He was enthusiastic about murder?"

"Well, his principal intent was to satirize the aesthetic theory of Immanuel Kant, but De Quincey did describe Cain, the first murderer recorded in the Bible, as 'a man of first-rate genius.' We shall see if the same level of genius has recently visited Grasmere."

The remainder of our journey north passed uneventfully, although the sun burst through the clouds about an hour after leaving London, promising a pleasant day ahead in the Lake District. At length, Holmes and I clambered into a cab in Windermere for the last leg of our excursion, which would take us the final nine miles to Grasmere. I had managed to pick up a map of the Lake District at the Oxenholme rail station, so that as we continued north, I was able to fill Holmes in on the various sites and scenery. After passing over the Troutbeck Bridge, we gradually turned west, and soon found ourselves almost on the banks of Lake Windermere itself, before passing through Ambleside and Rydal, then finding the River Rothay on our left before finally entering the bucolic village of Grasmere. As our cab came to a halt, Holmes immediately leapt out as I sat in a kind of daze, still endeavouring to take in the stupefying amount of beauty I had just witnessed.

Too much time in London had accustomed me to a hard world of buildings and business, and crowds of people hurrying to their next destination with nary a glance at their fellow humans. The rhythm of the city was like a steam-hammer metronome, all hustle and bustle, the affairs of Empire requiring a pace and energy that left no time for pause or reflection. But the Lake District was the antithesis of London. Gentle peaks rose next to softly burbling waters. The puffy white forms of sheep dotted hillsides, and the rare person that was seen moved with all the leisure of a Highland cow exploring a fresh field of clover. We entered Grasmere itself via a winding road framed by ancient stone walls, to the sound of joyous schoolchildren in their bright blue sweaters chasing a ball across an emerald field of grass. It was, quite simply, a world of almost unbearable beauty.

"Murder, Watson." I came to with a start, seeing Holmes's face staring at me from outside the cab.

"Right, of course!" I scrambled to collect my things. "Murder."

The cab had come to a halt outside the extremely modest Grasmere police station, and a moment later we were in the even more modest office of Chief Constable Alan Willadsen, who rose to greet us. He was a young man, perhaps not even thirty, with dark brown eyes and an apparently untamable cowlick in his light blond hair. His hands fluttered, his eyes shifted back and forth, and he gave every appearance of a man for whom the past few hours had been the most stressful of his life.

"Mr. Holmes! Dr. Watson! Thank you so much for coming! Thank you! Please sit down. If you would care to sit. Or we can stand. I'm entirely at your disposal whether we stand or sit. Thank you so much for coming!"

Holmes and I exchanged a glance, then Holmes reached for one of the plain wooden chairs next to the desk and I followed his lead.

"Perhaps we'll just sit a moment," began Holmes, "so you can fill us in on what's happened."

"Excellent!" Willadsen took his chair behind the desk. "That way we're all sitting. Most excellent, indeed. Yes."

Willadsen licked his dry lips as his gaze flickered between Holmes and myself.

"Calm yourself, Willadsen. What's done is done. Watson and I will do our utmost to assist you as best we can."

162

"Thank you! Yes indeed! Excellent! Most excellent! Thank you so much for coming!"

As Willadsen lapsed into silence, Holmes leaned across the desk and grasped Willadsen by the wrist, "I want you to get a hold of yourself and tell us what has happened. Your telegram said there had been a murder."

Swallowing hard, Willadsen only nodded, so Holmes continued. "Do you know who was murdered?"

"I do, yes," answered Willadsen. "Indeed, I do. Yes."

"Would you care to share the name of the unfortunate individual with us?"

"Mr. Percy Cholmondeley." Even uttering the name stirred Willadsen to new heights of agitation. He rose from his chair and began pacing behind it, wringing his hands. "Mr. Holmes, I pride myself on being a good Chief Constable. In my time in Grasmere, I have located or retrieved no fewer than two dozen lost pets. If I do say so myself, my familiarity with everyone in the village enables me to break up almost any pub fight with no damage to the participants or the pub itself. And just last month I was able to solve the mystery of the disappearing gingerbread. But this…"

Willadsen turned to us and spread his hands in supplication.

Holmes rose from his chair. "Perhaps if you could take us to the scene of the crime."

"Yes. The scene of the crime. Yes, indeed. It's not too far from here."

True enough, a walk of not more than five minutes was all that was needed to leave any trace of human activity behind us. As we entered a small copse of trees, Willadsen's pace slowed, and he gestured with his head that Holmes and I should venture deeper into the woods. Not fifty yards further on we came upon a most jarring sight. Two butterfly nets lay next to what I presumed was the murder victim, who was leaning against a tree and had been covered by a rough tarpaulin. Keeping his distance behind us, Willadsen explained the scene.

"I put the tarpaulin over him, Mr. Holmes," began Willadsen. "I didn't know what else to do. Then I sent a telegram to you."

"You left the body unguarded?" asked Holmes. At a helpless shrug from Willadsen, Holmes continued. "Who discovered it?"

"Jamie Goodison. Smart lad. Just turned ten years old last week. On his way to school, he took this way as a shortcut and…found what he found. He came straight to me, or at least he said he did. I told him not to tell anyone."

"And judging by what footprints I can observe, he has obeyed your injunction," said Holmes. "Curious. A lad of that age would usually be frantic to tell his friends about such a discovery."

"Mr. Holmes," Willadsen hesitated. "The poor boy was traumatized. He could barely speak when he came to me. And when he led me back here, I understood why. I knew right away that it was Mr. Cholmondeley, but…" Willadsen trailed off with a shake of his head.

"Very good, Willadsen," said Holmes. "Just stay where you are while Watson and I examine the body."

Being careful with every step he took, Holmes approached the slouched form beneath the tarpaulin as I followed behind him. With infinite care, he lifted the tarpaulin and pulled it from the corpse, revealing a sight that will stay with me until the day I die. It was a heavyset man of some sixty years of age, grey hair, with two flasks on the ground next to him, as well as some birding glasses nestled in his lap. A collecting box for butterflies was nearby, and it was here that the vision veered into the obscene and fantastical. His killing jar, one made of clear glass with a mass of what appeared to be white cotton wool stuffed into the bottom, had been tied to the poor man's face by a leather cord, covering both his mouth and nose. Worse than this, the loose tarpaulin which had covered him had not deterred various insects from descending upon his corpse for an easy meal. Even as Holmes and I looked on, various flies and ants were entering and leaving his eye sockets, and I observed Holmes's jaw clench as he took in this grotesque vision.

Ever the master of even the most disturbing situation, Holmes spoke without even turning. "Willadsen, I want you to fetch a cart or barrow so that we may convey Mr. Cholmondeley to the local doctor's office, where we might examine him more closely."

The words were scarcely out of Holmes's mouth before the sounds of the rapidly retreating Willadsen had faded into silence. Kneeling next to the corpse, Holmes quickly determined that both of the flasks were empty, as was the box for collecting butterflies. He then carefully examined the leather cord knotted around the killing jar, before using his penknife to cut it and removing the jar from Cholmondeley's face. Holmes waved his hand gently over the open top of the jar, cautiously sniffing the air.

"Potassium cyanide," he announced. "A popular means of disposing of insects among entomologists, but lethal to any living organism."

"In this case, Mr. Cholmondely," I added.

"An ugly way to die," said Holmes, "but the absence of any signs of struggle would indicate the following sequence of events. Mr. Cholmondeley armed himself for his butterfly hunting expedition with his weapons of choice, but having little success decided to sit down beneath this tree and drown his sorrows from these two flasks."

Holmes picked up one of the flasks and sniffed at the opening.

"Gin," he announced, "which apparently caused Mr. Cholmondeley to fall into an alcohol-induced slumber. It was then that some unknown passerby happened upon this scene and decided to relieve Mr. Cholmondeley of all his earthly troubles with the weapon at hand—a jarful of cyanide."

165

"Do you think the murder could possibly have been pre-meditated?" I asked.

"Not at all. Observe that this piece of leather cord used to secure the jar previously served to hang the birding glasses around Mr. Cholmondeley's neck. Our enterprising murderer simply took advantage of the materials at hand."

"Who would do such a thing?" I asked.

"Who indeed?" answered Holmes, pulling out his magnifying lens as he crouched down. "Let us see if a closer examination of the ground reveals anything."

Some ten minutes later, Holmes rose to his full height with a grumble. "Thanks to his substantial girth, the tracks of Mr. Cholmondeley are relatively easy to follow. I was also able to detect traces of what must be Willadsen's movements. Beyond that, nothing. The ground is simply too firm to retain any other impressions."

It was at that moment that we heard sounds of Willadsen returning with a cart to transport the body, and Holmes turned to me. "We shall have to enquire as to whether Mr. Cholmondeley had any known enemies or individuals who might benefit from his untimely demise. That can wait until we have had an opportunity to examine the body further. Not to impugn the abilities of rural practitioners, Watson, but if you could possibly assist in that examination, I would be most grateful."

Less than an hour later, the late Mr. Cholmondeley had been laid out on an examination table and I had been joined in the task of conducting the post-mortem by the elderly Dr. Spencer, whose contribution to the effort consisted largely of circling the table and muttering, "It's a bad business."

Chief Constable Willadsen refused to enter the room and was pacing up and down the corridor, while Holmes stood off to the side of the corpse and offered brief comments and suggestions regarding any recent abrasions, checking beneath the man's fingernails, and so on. In the end, we found nothing re-markable and settled on what had appeared to be apparent from the first—Mr. Cholmondeley had died from inhaling the va-pours of his own killing jar.

Following this, Holmes thought it might be best to settle Willadsen's nerves with a libation or two at the Grasmere Arms, and after half an hour it was a visibly relaxed Willadsen who answered Holmes's query as to whether Mr. Cholmondeley had any enemies. With a gentle shake of his head and another sip from his glass, Willadsen launched into his narrative.

"Where to begin, Mr. Holmes? The man seemed to posi-tively revel in the discomfort and pain of others. As best as I have been able to determine, he came into a small inheritance in Newcastle and moved here shortly thereafter. That was about a year ago. Apparently, he took a fancy to the sisters who run the Grasmere Gingerbread Shop, Agnes and Irene Nelson, but when they both rejected his attentions, his moral character be-gan to decline. He began drinking more and more heavily and took up the pursuit of butterfly hunting as a hobby. No one here seriously believed he had any interest in butterflies, but he used it as an excuse to traipse all over other people's property at all hours of the day. I can't tell you the number of complaints I've had about ruined cabbage patches and trampled rose bushes. I would try talking to him and I've fined him on several occasions for trespassing, but he would simply pay the fine and carry on as before. We almost came to blows at one point."

"Really?" Holmes looked across the table at Willadsen. "What manner of mischief caused that? Not a ruined field of daffodils, I hope."

Willadsen smiled at Holmes's remark, then began reciting Wordsworth from memory:

I wandered lonely as a cloud
That floats on high o'er vales and hills,
When all at once I saw a crowd,
A host, of golden daffodils.

Holmes softly applauded this brief recitation, before asking, "And your own poetic efforts. How are they coming along?"

Giving Holmes a rueful smile, Willadsen shook his head. "Doggerel, Mr. Holmes. The best I can manage is poorly rhymed doggerel. I have come to realize that it is one thing to appreciate beauty, but quite another to express it eloquently. I would just as soon move back to London save for the fact that…well, I'm sure you would agree that Grasmere does have its charms."

With that, Willadsen pulled a small notebook from his coat and set it before Holmes. "I don't know if this will be any help, but this is a record of all the disturbances in Grasmere since my arrival. Nothing of much consequence, as you will see, but please note the sheer number of incidents that involved Mr. Cholmondeley."

"Excellent, Willadsen." Holmes picked up the notebook and began leafing through it, his eyes scanning quickly every page. After a few moments of this, Holmes glanced up. "I note that the Grasmere Gingerbread Shop appears to be the scene of a number of recent altercations."

"Perhaps that's too strong a word," answered Willadsen. "Mr. Cholmondeley was in the habit of getting liquored up and then appearing in the shop just as they were closing. As I mentioned, he seemed to take great pleasure if he could somehow inconvenience or otherwise harass practically anyone in the village. But the principal target of his venom centered on the Gingerbread Shop, which is run by the two sisters who had rejected his advances. Lately, he had even begun making highly inappropriate comments to their niece, who is recently arrived in Grasmere and works in the shop as well."

"How recently?" asked Holmes.

"Two months ago. Apparently, her father died in a fishing accident on the Irish Sea and it was her two aunts who very kindly took her in."

"Ah," Holmes closed the notebook, "then perhaps we might venture to this Gingerbread Shop to see what else we can learn. But before we do that, let me ask you, Willadsen, have you formed any theory as to Mr. Cholmondeley's demise?"

"I have, Mr. Holmes, but I hesitate to even mention it for fear you will consider it too absurd to be remotely possible."

"Not at all," answered Holmes. "In my profession I have found it necessary to be open to even the most far-fetched theories until they have been proven false. What are you thinking?"

"I'm thinking..." Willadsen drained the remains of his glass and took a deep breath. "I'm thinking suicide."

Without looking I could almost feel Holmes's eyebrows arching upward. "Indeed? I will admit that's as bold a theory as I have ever encountered. What, pray tell, leads your suspicions in that direction?"

"With all due respect to the dead," continued Willadsen, "Mr. Cholmondeley was the most unpleasant human being I have ever encountered. It was as if some kind of evil worm writhed in his brain morning, noon, and night. When he saw beauty his first instinct was to destroy it."

"Hence his hobby of catching butterflies," I added.

"But not for science, nor even to admire their aesthetic beauty in death," returned Willadsen. "Simply to kill. To deprive others of their beauty and the butterflies themselves of their very lives."

"Very well," said Holmes, "but how does all that lead to a man deciding to not only kill himself, but to try and make it appear as if he was murdered?"

"I'm not going to pretend I can understand his motivation completely," answered Willadsen, "but I was thinking about the issue as I waited for you and Dr. Watson to arrive from London. It occurred to me that if Mr. Cholmondeley had recently been diagnosed with some form of fatal malady, or if he himself suspected that his end was near, he would be mortified at the thought of going out with a whimper. Instead, he would concoct

169

some form of monstrous scheme to inflict pain and misery even after he was gone. He would stage his own death, with the hope of making it appear that he had been murdered, with some perfectly innocent person then being convicted of the crime and quite possibly hanged."

"So that Mr. Cholmondeley would have his last laugh from the grave," I added.

"Exactly, Dr. Watson! That is precisely the sort of person he was."

Holmes leaned back in his chair and observed both Willadsen and I for some time as I saw his eyes shifting back and forth. At length, he rose from his chair and announced, "I fancy some gingerbread. Watson, can I tempt you at all?"

"Absolutely!" I answered, feeling more than a bit peckish.

Willadsen had risen from his chair at Holmes's words, and I could see an expression of excited anticipation in his face. "I'll take you straight there!" he announced. "As I mentioned to you, the shop is run by two sisters, Agnes and Irene Nelson, and it's their niece Euphemia who helps them out minding the counter. Given their unpleasant dealings with Mr. Cholmondeley, I thought it best to inform them of his demise, but swore them to secrecy regarding the matter."

This earned a sound of disapproval from Holmes, "Willadsen, in the future I would encourage you to follow the advice of Benjamin Franklin, who once astutely observed, 'Three can keep a secret, if two of them are dead.' But what's done is done. Please be so kind as to lead the way."

Our ensuing brisk stroll through town was accompanied by a few curious stares, so it was apparent that news of the murder had begun to make its way around the village. Whether this was due to the young boy who found the body, the doctor with whom I had conducted the post-mortem, or the Nelson sisters was impossible to guess, but murder has a way of making itself known, especially in small communities like Grasmere. We soon found ourselves entering the Grasmere Gingerbread Shop, and as we did so the counter-girl looked up at us in surprise, then returned her attention to the customer in front of her. She was a tiny thing, somewhere in her twenties, scarcely over five feet tall, and possessed of flaming red hair and bright blue eyes. Her cheeks and nose were dappled with freckles and her familiarity with Willadsen was clearly evident as she relieved the customer of sixpence and then boxed up some gingerbread and speedily tied it up with butcher's string before turning her full attention on us.

"Alan!" she exclaimed. "How lovely to see you! And you've brought friends!"

"Indeed, I have!" answered Willadsen. "Euphemia, may I introduce you to Sherlock Holmes and his colleague Dr. Watson. They've come from London to help…well, to—"

"Meddle in our affairs?" boomed a feminine voice from the back of the shop. This was immediately followed by the appearance of not one, but two formidable ladies who came strolling towards us with expressions like thunder. This then, was presumably Irene and Agnes Nelson, the purveyors of the Grasmere Gingerbread Shop, and their ample forms spoke of their dedication to sampling their product on what I presumed was a daily basis. They were clearly anything but pleased to see us, as Willadsen began wringing his hands nervously and began to explain.

"They're…well, what's happened with…I thought perhaps consulting with an experienced authority in such matters…I thought that…" Willadsen trailed off feebly, and there followed a prolonged silence broken only when one of the sisters wiped her hands on her apron and launched into a sustained monologue, aided and abetted by her sister who chimed in with "ayes" and "that's right" whenever the first sister required a breath to continue speaking.

"Percy Cholmondeley was a monster who deserved what happened to him and there's no one in Grasmere about to mourn the death of a wicked man that we're well rid of…*aye, that's*

171

right…from the moment he came here he wasn't right in the head and not a day passed that he didn't make himself more unwelcome…*absolutely, aye*…even propositioning both Irene and I on the very same day and skulking away like a whipped dog when we told him what we thought of him…*too true that*…then when poor Phemie arrived here after the death of her father it wasn't more than a few days before that evil man started looking at her in a way we did not like…*no, we did not*…and it was only Alan coming into the shop just last Thursday, was it Thursday?...*aye, so it was*…that Mr. Cholmondeley was overstaying his welcome here and Alan gave him quite a talking to which we were happy to see…*so we were*…and Mr. Cholmondeley shook his finger at us and told us, well, I wouldn't like to say what he actually said…*no, no*…but it was very threatening best you believe it and he told us we'd be singing a different tune once he became our landlord which gave Irene and I quite a shock…*so it did*…and now that he's dead I say let the Devil take his soul and may he burn in eternity…*aye absolutely*."

As this dual soliloquy came to a close, I wasn't quite sure how either I or Holmes would respond, so it was with some relief that I realized that Euphemia was holding out small pieces of gingerbread to both of us.

"Would you care for a sample?" she asked, as if the impassioned speech of her aunts had never occurred. Holmes and I both took her offering and as Holmes popped the piece of gingerbread in his mouth, I saw him savouring it with an air of appreciation that was uncommon to him when it came to the matter of food. At length, Holmes gave a satisfied sigh.

"Remarkable," he began. "Quite, quite delicious. I would describe its texture as being somewhere between a biscuit and a cake and managing to be both sweet and pleasantly spicy at the same time thanks to an abundance of ground ginger, although I believe I detect notes of cinnamon and nutmeg as well. Truly unique. Unlike any gingerbread I have ever encountered. My congratulations, ladies. It's a rare thing in life to experience perfection, but that is what your gingerbread is. Your recipe is perfection and nothing less."

With that, the thundercloud expressions of both sisters dissipated in an instant, and sunny smiles lit up both of their faces.

"Oh, it's not our recipe...*no, no*...it was our Aunt Sarah who invented it...*back in 1854 it was*...not that she opened this shop right away...*no, she didn't*...but people loved it so much and kept asking her to make it...*aye, they did*...tourists would come here and then take our gingerbread back to the bigger cities, so now here we are...*aye, here we are*."

This was followed by an awkward pause, after which one of the sisters turned to Euphemia.

"Well, don't just stand there. Get these lovely gentlemen some more gingerbread."

Holmes held up his hands. "No, no, we couldn't possibly take advantage of your very gracious hospitality—"

"You can and you will...*with our compliments*...how many pieces would suit you?"

"Then perhaps just two or three small pieces to take with us back to London," answered Holmes.

With that, the lightning fingers of Euphemia went to work and within seconds Holmes held in his hands a box of gingerbread and we were back out on the street with the highly discombobulated Willadsen.

"Did I hear you right, Mr. Holmes? You're planning on returning to London immediately?"

"Yes, I'm afraid so. Watson and I shall spend the night at the Grasmere Inn, but then must begin our journey back south in the morning. However, I do have one question for you. The sisters failed to go into specifics, so I will ask you directly. What was the nature of your most recent unpleasant interaction with Mr. Cholmondeley?"

This was a question that clearly discomfited Willadsen, and he hemmed and hawed for a moment before answering. "As you might appreciate, Mr. Holmes, a man in my position does come in for a reasonable amount of abuse from the local populace, especially young men in their cups late in the evening. I'm used to it and accept it with as much good nature as I can manage. However, when I see a perfectly innocent person being subjected to such abuse, I simply cannot abide it. After making a drunken spectacle of himself with the sisters, I intervened so that they could close up the store. I thought that would be the end of it, but…"

"To point a finer point on it," said Holmes, "you came upon Mr. Cholmondeley speaking inappropriately to Euphemia Nelson."

The colour immediately rose in Willadsen's face as he cleared his throat. "That I did. Miss Nelson was on her way home and Mr. Cholmondeley caught up with her just outside the postmaster's. I will not repeat what I overheard, but once I had seen Euphemia on her way, yes, Mr. Cholmondeley and I had a rather spirited exchange, which ended with him threatening me in no uncertain terms."

"Would the postmaster be able to confirm this?" asked Holmes.

"I expect so, yes."

"Perhaps there was another witness or two in the vicinity?"

"I can't recall very clearly…I was in a somewhat heated frame of mind, Mr. Holmes, but quite possibly, yes."

At this, Holmes turned his eyes down the street and we became aware that several of the good citizens of Grasmere had gathered and were staring in our direction.

"Apparently, news of the death of Mr. Cholmondeley is spreading rapidly," said Holmes.

"Good Lord!" I detected a note of panic in Willadsen's voice. "This will make its way to Windermere and who knows where else?"

"Then you must prepare yourself for the arrival of the press, Willadsen," I offered. "Take it from me, they live for bizarre cases like this. In fact, the more macabre, the better."

"Mr. Holmes..." I could see Willadsen desperately trying to gather his scattered thoughts, "...could you possibly...if you might be able to...with all of your experience, perhaps you could handle any questions."

"As Chief Constable," began Holmes, "the press will be most interested in your opinion. Besides, as I mentioned, Watson and I will be returning to London as I have an appointment with my brother Mycroft tomorrow evening."

"But Mr. Holmes! The murder! Can you offer me any kind of guidance at all?"

"Call on me at our hotel in the morning before we leave. I shall then give you my opinion on the matter. Come along, Watson."

As was typical of Holmes, his long stride soon outpaced my own, and in truth I slowed my pace even further to take in the spectacular vista surrounding me. The sun was setting behind verdant hills, the sky has turned various shades of violet and orange, and the gentlest of summer zephyrs brought a fresh breeze to my cheeks. Life was beautiful, even if my thoughts were of a much more dismal shade. It was abundantly evident that Willadsen was smitten with the young Euphemia, and every leering remark to which Cholmondeley had subjected the poor girl had fired the rage building in Willadsen's heart. The threats to the Nelson sisters and his own well-being had only stoked those flames, and when the opportunity presented itself to rid the community of Cholmondeley, Willadsen had taken it. By the time I got to our hotel room, Holmes had already lit a pipe and was deep in thought as wisps of smoke made their way to the ceiling.

"Well, Watson, what do you make of it?"

Knowing that Holmes would ask me this, I had my answer ready. "Suicide, obviously. Just as Willadsen deduced. No question about it."

Holmes stared at me, then removed his pipe from his mouth. "Fascinating. Would you care to explain further?"

"Come now, Holmes. We both know very well what happened."

"Enlighten me."

"Chief Constable Willadsen may be a failure as a poet, but he could return to London and make his way onto any West End stage he pleased. Whether it be Shakespeare or Gilbert & Sullivan, I feel certain he would excel in any role. The man is a consummate actor. His apparent nerves and squeamishness since we arrived have been an act first to last."

"Then he is our murderer?"

"Of course! Did he have the motive? Most assuredly. The fact that he is quite taken with Euphemia Nelson is obvious, so he would feel duty-bound to protect her honour. Then he was threatened in public by Mr. Cholmondeley in front of witnesses. This would come out at any inquest, as would the fact that the ground immediately around Cholmondeley's body showed signs of only two pairs of footprints, the victim's and Willadsen's."

"I follow you so far," said Holmes, "but why would he summon me from London to investigate the crime if he was the perpetrator?"

"What greater proof of his innocence could there be than calling in Sherlock Holmes? Would a guilty man do such a thing? Of course not, therefore he must be innocent. That's what he's counting on, and I say we play along rather than send the poor man to the gallows."

"Hmm..." Holmes rose from his chair and produced his penknife. With an easy motion he cut the string on the gingerbread box, opened it, and offered me a slice. "Perhaps a piece of gingerbread might clear your thoughts."

"Then you don't agree?" I asked.

"I do not."

"Are you suggesting...?" My thoughts were in a whirl as I tried to reorder the sequence of events in some manner that would make sense. And then, it all came to me in a rush, the way a magnifying lens may gather the gentle rays of the sun and focus them into a searing pinpoint of light. "The Nelson sisters! Of course! Not only did Cholmondeley threaten them, he threatened their niece as well! Quite rightly, they decided that the air of Grasmere would be decidedly sweeter without the odious presence of Mr. Cholmondeley. They chanced upon the opportunity to murder him and took full advantage of it!"

"A plausible theory," began Holmes, "and I assure you that I shouldn't wish to fall afoul of the formidable Nelson sisters, but again no."

"Why not?"

"I would draw your attention to the curious incident of the footprints at the murder scene." As I gazed at Holmes in mystification, he continued. "As you rightly observed, the heavy-set Cholmondeley left his footprints and the lightly built Willadsen left only faint traces. Both sisters being nearer in size to Cholmondeley than Willadsen, presumably they would have left clear footprints as well. But we're forgetting one more presence at the scene, young Jamie Goodison, the ten-year-old boy who found the body. Not a sign of him anywhere for the simple reason that he is only a child and too small and light to leave any impression on the earth."

"You don't think he had anything to do with it, do you?" I asked.

"Of course not. But cast about in your mind for any other person we encountered today who would be too small and light to leave any kind of footprint behind."

"Euphemia!" I gaped at Holmes. "Surely not! She's such a tiny thing."

"A tiny thing who is madly in love with Willadsen, a fact that he has yet to fully appreciate. She had the motive, saw her opportunity, and took it."

"But how can you say such a thing? She was pleasant enough to Willadsen, but she was pleasant enough to us as well. There was nothing said between them that would indicate any kind of intense passion on her part."

"Love may speak its mind," continued Holmes, "as so many poets have expressed with great eloquence, but passion goes beyond words. If you had observed closely, when young Euphemia looked at Willadsen, there arose at the base of her throat a slight blushing effect, a capillary response to his presence quite out of her control. For all of our pretensions, human beings are still animals, and that response in the female signals to the male that his attentions will be most welcome."

"For God's sake, Holmes..."

"You may take it from me, she did not stray far when Willadsen rescued her from Cholmondeley's attentions outside the postmaster's. When she witnessed the confrontation between the two men, her reaction would have been one of absolute fury, wanting nothing more than to fly to the defense of the man with whom she is in love. However, being a woman and not possessed of the size or strength to physically assault Cholmondeley, she could only fume in impotent anger...until Providence itself put the drunk and unconscious Cholmondeley in her path only days later. It was a heaven-sent opportunity, and it was an opportunity that she took."

I shook my head at Holmes's words. "I see where you're coming from, but I'm sorry, I'm just not convinced."

"No? Observe." Holmes took the string that had been used to tie up the gingerbread box and set it before me. He then drew from his pocket the leather cord that had secured the killing jar to Cholmondeley's face and put it next to the string. "I would draw your attention to the knots."

Looking at both of the knots, it was instantly apparent that they were identical, as Holmes continued. "There are a variety of knots favoured by fishermen. This is known as the Palomar Knot, prized for the speed with which it can be executed. As we learned, Euphemia Nelson's late father was a fisherman, and I have no doubt that she learned this at her father's knee. Quite practical when tying up packages…and for other uses."

I looked up at Holmes, then down at the two knots, the truth of Holmes's words settling into me. A moment later, Holmes had swept both the string and the leather cord into his pocket.

"It has been a long day for both of us, Watson, and not without its exertions. We've an early rise and long journey before us tomorrow, so I propose that we retire early. I'll have a word with Willadsen before we depart."

Exhausted as I was thanks to my early morning with Mrs. Higgins, I still had trouble dropping off to sleep. The implications of everything Holmes had said weighed heavily on me, and the vision of the insects crawling in and out of Mr. Cholmondeley's eye sockets was not one to encourage peaceful slumber. Still, I clearly managed to fall asleep because I awoke to Holmes shaking me gently by the shoulder as morning light streamed through the window.

"Our cab awaits, old boy. Shift yourself and we'll be on our way."

"Have you spoken to Willadsen?" I asked.

Holmes glanced out our window. "It would appear he has been unavoidably detained. No matter. In fact, the fewer words, the better."

Ten minutes later, Holmes and I exited the hotel to find our cab just outside, along with a sizable crowd of people awaiting our appearance. Sure enough, Chief Constable Willadsen had been encircled by assorted townsfolk, and I spied the Nelson sisters and their niece Euphemia standing off to the side as three gentlemen of the press approached Holmes with their notebooks open and pencils ready. As expected, word of Mr.

Cholmondeley's gruesome demise had spread beyond Grasmere, and would doubtless spread further in the coming days. Holmes stopped the three newspapermen in their tracks with a raised hand.

"Gentlemen, as much as I would like to tarry and answer all of your questions, I'm afraid that my friend Dr. Watson and I have a train to catch in Windermere. However, I will make a short statement related to this case and my findings. It was Chief Constable Willadsen who contacted me to request my assistance, and when I enquired as to his opinion of the case, he stated that he felt that Mr. Cholmondeley had died by his own hand with the intended purpose of making it appear as if he had been murdered. Shortly after this, I questioned my colleague Dr. Watson on the same point and found that he agreed with Chief Constable Willadsen's view of the case. Having examined all of the available evidence and given the matter my due consideration, I feel quite confident in issuing my own verdict, which coincides with that of my colleagues—Mr. Cholmondeley died by suicide. Nothing more, nothing less."

A buzz of excitement went around the assembled crowd as the gentlemen from the press scribbled frantically in their notebooks, and a moment later Holmes and I were in our cab. Motioning Willadsen to approach, Holmes had a quiet word in his ear, and then we were off at a pace calculated to get us to Windermere in time to catch our train back to London. It had all happened so fast that I was only able to manage my first question when we were a good way down the road.

"What did you say to Willadsen?"

"Nothing much. Just a gentle word of encouragement regarding his prospects with Euphemia Nelson."

"The murderess."

"The very same. I suspect she would rank quite high in Thomas De Quincey's assessment of various murderers throughout history. As De Quincey wrote, 'If once a man indulges himself in murder, very soon he comes to think little of robbing; and from robbing he comes next to drinking and Sabbath-breaking, and from that to incivility and procrastination.' Let us hope that Miss Euphemia Nelson's indulgence doesn't lead her down such a dark path."

I sat back in my seat for a moment, looking out at the passing scenery, then felt duty-bound to state the readily obvious. "Holmes, we have sanctioned the murder of Percy Cholmondeley."

"Indeed we have. And what of it? I am interested in only two things—truth and justice. We were able to discover the truth, and I am satisfied that the actions of Miss Nelson were justified. Justice is not the sole province of bewigged old men in courtrooms, Watson. Justice belongs to all of us. It is when good people stand by and let wickedness prosper that any civilization begins its inexorable decline. Miss Nelson may have been motivated by her tender feelings for Willadsen, but she struck a blow for all of the inhabitants of Grasmere. Let us hope that when we are put in a similar position, that we would do likewise."

"All the same, Holmes, I suspect that the English legal community would take exception to your point of view."

"The wealthy and powerful men of England devoted to protecting the interests of other wealthy and powerful men? No doubt. But that is not justice and it would be a heresy against the truth to declare it as such. Am I suggesting anarchy? By no means. But a society in which every member feels they have a vested interest in justice taking place? Yes. A thousand times yes. So, I have no compunction in saying that I hope Miss Nelson and Chief Constable Willadsen have many pleasant gingerbread-filled years ahead of them."

At this, I couldn't help but smile, and to my astonishment Holmes proceeded to reach into his pocket to retrieve two pieces of Grasmere gingerbread wrapped in paper. He handed one of the pieces to me and we raised our gingerbread in a toast.

"To the happy couple," announced Holmes.

"Hear, hear!" I agreed.

And with that, we both fell silent and devoted our attention to the quite excellent gingerbread of Grasmere.

The End.

The Adventure of the Mysterious Benefactor

In stark contrast to the other stories in this volume, this tale is not meant to be a faithful Canonical pastiche in any way, shape, or form. It is a whimsical take on Holmes and Watson during the holiday season, and it was first published back in the Pleistocene Era in the pages of the late, lamented, Mike Shayne Mystery Magazine. *Christmas is a magical time of year for both children and adults, and while it presents its own mysteries to those of a skeptical mind, sometimes it is best to put the mystery to the side, and simply enjoy the magic.*

It was a bitter winter's day towards the end of 1889 that found Sherlock Holmes and myself gratefully ensconced in our rooms in Baker Street, each engaged in his own individual pursuit. Outside, an Arctic chill had descended upon London and with each blast of frigid air that rattled our windowpanes I found myself taking renewed comfort in the warmth and light that our well-stoked fire afforded. I was in the midst of reviewing my notes concerning some of Holmes's more intriguing cases of the past year, when a heavy tread upon the stairs foretold the arrival of an unexpected visitor.

The resounding knock that echoed through our chambers caused Holmes to look up sharply from the chemical experiment in which he was engaged, and I moved quickly to open the door. As I did, I was greeted by an apparition that fully filled our doorway, a giant of a man rendered even taller by the shiny top hat he wore. Our visitor, doubtless accustomed to the looks of slack-jawed wonder similar to the one I was wearing, stepped into our rooms without invitation and casually flicked off the few snowflakes that had had the temerity to make their way to his collar as he surveyed our quarters in a cool, unhurried manner.

At length, his gaze lit on my friend Sherlock Holmes and,

removing his hat, he executed a sweeping bow. "*Mr*. Sherlock Holmes," he boomed, "it is indeed a pleasure."

"And a pleasure it is to meet you as well," replied Holmes, "Mr. Morgan Clarkwell."

Our visitor seemed delighted by Holmes's response. "Wonderful, Mr. Holmes! You are everything I expected. Pray tell your line of deduction."

"I'm sure my explanation can wait until you've made yourself comfortable before the fire," answered Holmes. "Watson, be so good as to fetch our guest a brandy. I'm sure he must be chilled after his journey."

"You are very kind," said Clarkwell as he removed his coat. "It is somewhat bracing out there."

After our guest was seated with his brandy, he repeated his query to Holmes, who shrugged slightly from his armchair before replying. "It was quite elementary, Mr. Clarkwell. Upon your entrance you made a close scrutiny of our rooms before addressing, or even looking at me. I observed your gaze as it travelled the length of our mantelpiece, lingered thoughtfully on the remains of our recent lunch, and at length examined with some interest the mass of papers which Watson has seen fit to strew about the floor.

"Long experience has borne out the fact to me that such behaviour is only observable in three professions, namely: housekeepers, policemen, and private detectives. Now, if you'll pardon my saying so, Mr. Clarkwell, you haven't the look of a housekeeper, and although I am not familiar with all of the members of Scotland Yard, I surely would have noticed a man of your stature by this time. Thus, the latter choice was the only one open to me, a choice strengthened by the recollection that only last month I read of a case solved by London's second private consulting detective, a Mr. Morgan Clarkwell.

"Marvellous!" cried our visitor as he clapped his hands together. "I'm glad to see that the reports of your powers have not been exaggerated, Mr. Holmes."

"You're too kind," replied Holmes softly, although it was evident that he was pleased at Clarkwell's words. "Tell me, Mr. Clarkwell, what decided you on a career as a private detective?"

"Dr. Watson," answered Clarkwell, with a nod in my direction.

"Indeed?" Holmes appeared serious, but I could read a faint look of amusement in his eyes.

"Yes," continued Clarkwell. "Initially, I was strictly an insurance investigator, and only took on private work for my friends or close family. My interest in the profession gradually deepened, and I'll readily admit that my head was more than slightly turned by the doctor's glowing accounts of your successes, Mr. Holmes."

Here it was my turn to redden at Clarkwell's praise and I hurried to the replenishing of his glass lest my embarrassment become too obvious. As I did so, I was much relieved to hear Holmes pick up the thread of conversation.

"I trust then, Mr. Clarkwell, that it is a problem of some importance that not only forces you out in this weather, but necessitates the consulting of another private detective."

At Holmes's words Clarkwell seemed to recall the reason for his visit and a faint look of worry came into his eyes. "Yes, Mr. Holmes, I do consider it a pressing problem, and I only hope you won't laugh at its apparent triviality. It has been weighing on my mind all this month, and as time has almost run out, I decided to swallow my pride and seek your opinion."

He looked up for a moment, but Holmes's face was an impassive mask. "Go on," said my friend.

"Well," resumed Clarkwell, "it concerns the 25th of December, tomorrow, that is. Every year, or almost every year, someone breaks into our home and leaves things, and only on that precise date."

"What do you mean 'leaves things?'" queried Holmes. "What sort of things?"

"Various gifts and trinkets," responded Clarkwell. "Every

185

year it's something – a tie, shoes, perfume for the wife, a tin of meat for the cat. And always gaily wrapped too."

"And this unknown person or persons never takes anything?" pressed Holmes. "Only leaves the gifts?"

"Yes," Clarkwell reached for his brandy and I observed a perceptible trembling of his hand. "And the damnable thing is, he always seems to know precisely what we need. Just last year the wife and I were discussing the possibility of buying a new tea cosy and perhaps a larger toast rack, and what did we find on the 25th upon arising but those very things!"

"The fiend!" I muttered, scarcely able to believe the story I was hearing.

Holmes ignored my outburst and leaned forward as he questioned Clarkwell further. "Surely you've attempted some measures to halt this phenomenon?"

"Of course I have," replied Clarkwell, "but to no avail. Double-locked doors and windows are no hindrance to this sort of man. Twice I took it into my head to stay up all might and capture him in the act, but although I doused all the lights and skillfully concealed myself, he failed to show on both occasions."

"You mean to say," said Holmes, whose eyes were glittering excitedly under half-closed lids, "that he knows when you are sleeping and he knows when you're awake?"

"Yes," answered Clarkwell. "You put it well, Mr. Holmes. It seems there is little that he doesn't know. The only clue I can give you is perhaps the most curious thing of all regarding this affair. Last year, while the wife was trying out the new tea cosy I took myself outside for a breath of fresh air and found to my surprise a fair sprinkling of snow on our front porch. I say this was curious, Mr. Holmes, for on the previous evening I had swept the porch clean and there had been no fresh snowfall during the night. A moment's reflection made it clear to me that the snow must have fallen from our roof and, intrigued and perhaps more than a bit suspicious, I immediately fetched a ladder and clambered up it.

"Well, Mr. Holmes," continued Clarkwell after a swallow of brandy had steadied his nerves, "I hope you will continue to regard me as a sane man when I relate to you what I found. I found footprints on the roof, sir."

"Footprints?" repeated Holmes. "A man's or a woman's?"

Clarkwell paused to glance at both of us in turn and his voice sank to a throaty whisper as he answered, "Mr. Holmes, they were the footprints of a gigantic reindeer!"

I cannot accurately recount the effect that Clarkwell's words had on us. An ominous silence filled the room and I felt the hair on the back of my neck fairly stand on end. Clarkwell, whose features bore evidence of an almost paralytic fear, turned his eyes beseechingly to Holmes. "You must believe me!"

"Certainly I believe you, Mr. Clarkwell," replied Holmes in a soothing voice. "Is there anything else you wish to add?"

"No, nothing," answered Clarkwell, his unease fading rapidly under Holmes's studied calm. "That's all there is, as if that isn't enough. The wife, she's convinced we're under some ancient family curse. Mind you, I don't go for that nonsense, but I must admit I'm fairly well stumped. I only hope you can shed some light on this, Mr. Holmes. If you can't..." Clarkwell trailed off, and he suddenly seemed like a very weary and broken man.

"Have no fear, Mr. Clarkwell," Holmes reassured him. "I shall be delighted to look into your case. If Watson here will deign to lend me a hand, I daresay we'll have some promising news for you by tomorrow."

"I'd be very grateful, Mr. Holmes," said Clarkwell as relief shone in his eyes. The two men stood up to shake hands and, after gathering his coat and hat, we soon heard Morgan Clarkwell's footsteps retreating ponderously down our stairs.

"I don't know about this, Holmes," I began as soon as we were alone. "It seems the work of a madman."

"You think so?" Holmes returned to his armchair, and after repeated attempts managed to get his old briar pipe lit. "It is a

187

singular thing, Watson, that Clarkwell should mention the 25th of December as the date of these occurrences. That's the very day when you invariably leave me a nicely wrapped gift, usually a tin of tobacco or some such thing."

"Surely you're mistaken, Holmes," I replied with a start. "It is you who leaves me something, a Clark Russell sea novel wrapped in a festive red bow last year if I recall."

At my words, Holmes abandoned his speculative air and stared at me with a look that fairly froze the blood in my veins. "Good God, Watson, do you mean it wasn't you who left me the bow rosin for my violin last year?"

"Why no, Holmes," I replied with some confusion.

"And I have never bought you a Clark Russell sea novel in my life." Holmes slowly sank back into his armchair, but every fibre of his being was taut with excitement. "Deep waters, Watson," mused Holmes as he turned a somber eye towards me. "Deep waters, indeed."

I had scarcely time to collect my thoughts on the matter before Holmes had sprung out of his chair and quickly donned his coat and hat. "Surely you're not venturing out in this weather?" I began.

"Action is what's called for Watson, and it's action that shall be taken. I have a fair idea what's behind all this, but one wire to Inspector Lestrade at Scotland Yard will make it all clear." And with that, he was gone.

Holmes returned a short time later in a state of great excitement, lit his briar, and nervously paced the length of our rooms again and again. "It's unthinkable," he muttered to himself from time to time, but I was unable to get any further response from him until, at length, a rap sounded at our door. Holmes sprang towards it like a man possessed and without a word grabbed the telegram from the delivery boy while handing him a tip that I saw to be clearly excessive. Holmes left the door ajar as he feverishly ripped open the envelope and devoured its contents at a glance.

"Ha! Look at this, will you, Watson?" beamed Holmes as he threw the wire towards me. "I thought as much!"

Picking the wire off the floor, I read:

Holmes,
Re your query. Have received many gifts on date indicated. Occasionally marked "From St. Nick." Woolly jumper last year.

Lestrade

"What does it all mean, Holmes?" I asked.

"It means, Watson, that this is more than the work of some idle philanthropist. Can you not see the pattern?"

I confessed that I could not.

"What do we have in common with Morgan Clarkwell and Inspector Lestrade? We are all investigators or detectives of one sort or another." Holmes paused to relight his briar. "I sense a malignant presence behind all this, Watson. I believe the Professor is on the move again."

"Not Moriarty!" I exclaimed.

"Yes, Moriarty," replied Holmes through tight lips.

"But perhaps it's not what it seems, Holmes," I began, as an idea flashed through my brain. "Perhaps after a year of crime and villainy he wishes to make amends of a sort to his pursuers. You yourself have remarked upon his perverse personality. I shouldn't be surprised if he finds something terribly amusing at the thought of giving his arch-foes year-end presents."

Holmes eyed me curiously for a moment before breaking into a delighted laugh. "Excellent, Watson! You have surveyed the evidence, applied known personality traits of the perpetrator, and arrived at a highly probable solution. I'm gratified that my lessons of the past few years have not gone totally unheeded."

I was on the verge of uttering something modest and unassuming when, to my great chagrin, Holmes continued speaking. "I'm afraid, however, that I don't agree with your theory as it ignores the fact that the overriding characteristic of Moriarty's personality is a complete and total incapacity of any action even remotely good. I suspect a far more evil design."

I was eager to hear this theory, my own being so presumptively dismissed, but Holmes demurred. "Not now, Watson. The day's events have proved interesting thus far, but I fear there is little to do until later this evening. I suggest a bit of dinner at Simpson's over which I might give you my views on the case."

I hastily agreed to this most judicious plan, and it wasn't long before we were comfortably seated at Simpson's, a most palatable pair of beefsteaks before us. Holmes lingered distractedly as he began talking.

"You must understand, Watson, that Professor Moriarty is a man lost in evil. Every word he speaks, every action he takes, no matter how innocent it may appear, must be scrutinized closely. So, we have his latest scheme, leaving annual gifts for the detectives of London. We must ask ourselves two questions. How does he do it? And why? Clarkwell mentioned reindeer footprints on his roof. What does that suggest to you?"

"I really couldn't say," I replied.

"Come now, Watson," urged my friend. "Think! What sort of footprints would a reindeer leave?"

"Why, cloven hoofprints," I answered.

"Bravo, Watson!" said Holmes. "Cloven hoofprints, indeed. When Clarkwell mentioned those, my thoughts turned immediately towards Moriarty, for cloven hoofprints clearly represent the devil and on the rooftop means precisely that. The devil, in this case personified by Professor Moriarty, on top. Lestrade's wire clinched the matter when he mentioned that his gifts sometimes bore the message 'from St. Nick.' As you're no doubt aware, 'Old Nick' has long been an alias for the Devil, much like Satan, Lucifer, or Beelzebub, and Moriarty, somewhat carried away by the largesse of his gift giving, saw fit to amend 'Old Nick' to 'St. Nick.'"

"Wonderful, Holmes!" I exclaimed.

"And if all that weren't enough, the hoofprints on the roof also presented a method of entry that Clarkwell didn't think of, namely, the chimney."

"But Holmes," I protested, "I can't imagine a man of the Professor's age and build clambering up and down chimneys."

"Nor can I," agreed my friend. "Instead, I envision two or three highly trained monkeys completing the task. Moriarty has merely to attach replica cloven feet to the monkeys, give them the gifts, and send them on their way."

I stopped midway through my meal, momentarily sickened at the thought of so much genius being used to such an evil purpose. "But why, Holmes?" I asked.

"Why?" Holmes smiled thinly in reply. "The answer is obvious. Being detectives, we shall soon begin to question the origin of these gifts. Like Clarkwell, our only clue will be the cloven hoofprints left on our roof. What would your reaction be, Watson, if one of your fellow physicians should come to you with such as tale?"

"Why, I should say he was…" I stopped, and a tremor ran through me as I realized the implication of my next word. "…mad."

"Yes, Watson, insane," agreed Holmes. "As detectives, we serve an important public function. Oftentimes, it is our testimony alone that either frees a man or consigns him to the gallows. The responsibility is so great, that men such as yourself, Clarkwell, Lestrade, or I would surely remove ourselves from the public arena should we ever begin to doubt our sanity. Do I speak for you, Watson?"

"Why, certainly Holmes!" I replied vigorously. "For the public safety if nothing else!"

"Precisely," nodded Holmes. "If, on the other hand, any of us should refuse to take this honourable course, I assure you we should only have to wait for one of Moriarty's cronies to be brought to trial and our secret would shortly be out. I imagine only a few questions from even the most unskilled barrister regarding these mysterious gifts would be enough to ruin any detective's credibility forever."

I pushed my plate from me and sat back in my chair, overwhelmed at the enormity of the scheme that Moriarty had embarked upon. Within a few years he would have laid to rest everyone who presented the least threat to him. It was a plan only a genius could have conceived. Or a madman.

As I pondered further, my mind began to reel at the possibilities, and it seemed for a moment as if the very corners of the universe were about to converge upon us. I started from my reverie as I felt Holmes's strong grip on my arm and I slowly raised my eyes to meet his steely gaze.

"Steady on, Watson," my friend's reassuring words came across the table. "We've found him out in time. I daresay it will be the Professor who is in for a surprise this year."

I was cheered enormously by Holmes's words and attacked my steak with renewed fervour. London, I reflected, was surely fortunate to have a man such as Sherlock Holmes within its environs. After finishing our meal, we quickly made our way back to Baker Street with the aim of formulating a plan to lay the Professor by his heels that very evening. Upon entering our rooms, however, we both immediately shrank back towards the door at the sight of a tall, stooped figure who stood by our window, calmly observing the street below.

"Do come in, Holmes," said the figure. "I've been expecting you." As he slowly turned towards us, his high-domed forehead gleamed faintly in the evening light and I shuddered involuntarily as I felt Holmes stiffen by my side.

"Moriarty," breathed Holmes, his voice low with menace.

"Very good, Holmes," rejoined Moriarty. "I'm comforted to see that you have lost none of your keen deductive faculties."

Holmes made no reply to this brazen insult even as I furtively patted my pocket for my service revolver and cursed its absence.

"Come now, gentlemen," continued Moriarty. "I won't have you standing on ceremony for me. Please make yourselves comfortable. Delightful quarters you have here, Holmes, although perhaps a trifle less immaculate than one would wish." To illustrate his point, Moriarty drew his finger across the windowsill and clucked disapprovingly at the dust it collected. Holmes and I had by now edged warily further into the room, and the detective finally spoke to his arch-foe.

"Perhaps we'll have you round on one of your days off to tidy up, Professor, since it excites your interest so." Moriarty's eyes merely glittered in reply and my friend continued, "What is it you want, Professor?"

"Want?" Moriarty raised his eyebrows slightly and his head began to slowly oscillate in that peculiar fashion of his that was more reptilian than human. "I wish information, Holmes. It has come to my attention that you are investigating the mysterious gift-giving that takes place annually on the 25th of December."

"How do you know that?" asked Holmes.

"Come, come, Holmes," chided Moriarty, "you know my methods. Is what I hear true?"

"You know it is," replied Holmes. "The game is up Professor Moriarty, or should I say, 'St. Nick?'"

"Ah, I see. You suspect me of being 'St. Nick.'" The rapidity of Moriarty's head-weaving increased, and his features struggled to contort themselves into something resembling a smile. "Holmes, this is too delicious. I must say, I am flattered that you consider me capable of a scheme of worldwide magnitude."

"Worldwide?" echoed Holmes, a skeptical look on his face.

"Yes," continued Moriarty. "If you had widened the scope of your investigation a trifle, you would have discovered that this phenomenon is not confined to England. Every 25th of December, households around the world are showered with gifts of every shape and form. Mind you," and here a furrow creased Moriarty's brow, "I myself have never once received anything, aside from the occasional lump of coal left on my desk, doubtless through some oversight. Still, the enormity of the task is worthy of admiration. Nearly ninety million homes are visited in a twenty-four-hour period."

"And if not you, Professor, then who?" enquired Holmes.

"I wish I knew," replied Moriarty. "Like you, I have heard rumours of this 'St. Nick' but little else. The only other point of interest that I've been able to unearth is that if the night he makes his rounds is an especially foggy one, a small red light can be seen moving over the city at tremendous speed. I'm afraid I can tell you little else."

"It's of no consequence," answered Holmes with some vehemence. "Just as you'll meet your end, Professor, so shall this 'St. Nick' meet his."

"You mean you intend to try to apprehend him?" The prospect of this seemed to please Moriarty no end. "My dear Holmes, simple mathematics will inform you that if a man is capable of visiting ninety million homes within a twenty-four-hour span, then he spends less than one-thousandth of a second at each of them. And the great Sherlock Holmes is going to capture this man? Oh, it is wonderful, Holmes, simply wonderful!"

To my immense surprise, Moriarty then proceeded to twirl a complete circle in apparent delight, clapping his hands all the while. He followed this performance with an obscene high-pitched giggle, before moving suddenly towards our door and disappearing through it, his mocking cackle drifting back to us as he clattered noisily down the stairs. Holmes made no effort to stop the Professor, but instead turned towards the fire and gazed into it for some time in gloomy silence.

"Chin up, Holmes," I ventured at last with a forced show of cheer. "Perhaps Moriarty is still having us on."

Holmes never moved his eyes from the fire as he spoke in a calm voice. "No, Watson. The Professor is many things, but he is not fool enough to regale me with such a tale in my own home were it not the truth. This 'St. Nick' undoubtedly exists and he is as much a mystery to Moriarty as he is to me."

Holmes's depression deepened steadily throughout the evening until he was deep into one of his black moods. Picking up his violin and cradling it like a child, he began to play a haunting, melancholy air, and it was to these mournful strains that I eventually slipped into unconsciousness. It seemed I had hardly closed my eyes, however, before I felt my shoulder being vigorously shaken and I awoke with a start to find Holmes's grey eyes a scant few inches from my own.

"Come, Watson," he whispered, "the game is afoot!"

Groggily, I stumbled to my feet and observed that it was nearly midnight.

"A man can take defeat lying down," Holmes continued, "or he can face what may come on his own two feet. We, Watson, shall stand to the last!"

"But Holmes," I protested, "where are we going?"

"Up on the housetop, quick, quick, quick," replied Holmes as he threw on his Inverness. "Then down through the chimney with 'St. Nick.'"

Following Holmes's lead, we travelled through the attic and edged out cautiously through a small door that led to the roof. The footing was treacherous, a light snow aiding matters not in the least, but at length we both reached the chimney and paused in our exertions to catch our breath. Below us, London lay spread out like a vast fairy wonderland. Soft yellow lights twinkled in the distance, while the newly fallen snow swathed the land in a blanket of beauty and innocence. The only sound was that of a single horse-drawn carriage moving slowly down the street in muffled cadence. After some minutes of this tranquil view, I felt Holmes turn slightly towards me.

"What is it?" I asked.

"There's a north wind coming," replied Holmes as he pointed in that direction.

I shifted my view to the north and felt only the faintest possible breeze caress my cheek. I was about to question Holmes on this point when I felt a single finger upon my lips and the question died in my throat. In a moment, the breeze had become a gust, and as I glanced at Holmes I saw his unblinking eyes staring into the inky night, for what, God only knew.

My heart had scarcely time to quicken before a sudden whirlwind swept down upon the city. Desperately, I sought to keep my balance on the slick tiles of the roof as the gale howled around us, sweeping my bowler hat from my head, and to my dismay, sending it spinning down the street after the vortex. Holmes, unmindful of his own safety, was flailing wildly at the air as if battling some unseen foe and his frenzied shouts were unintelligible. I gazed helplessly at my friend, wondering how I could possibly aid him when, with one final icy blast, the storm suddenly left us. Silence fell quickly, the only sound the ragged breathing of Holmes and myself, but in my delirium I imagined I could hear the wind mocking our futile efforts, the words "Ho-Ho-Ho" sounding vaguely to my ears.

The light dusting of snow that had blown up slowly settled upon us, and as I struggled to regain my equilibrium, I saw Holmes sagging nearby on the chimney, a pain-stricken look on his face.

"I have failed, Watson," his voice was barely audible. "Failed utterly."

These words from the great detective brought an uncontrollable lump to my throat, and I was only glad at that moment that I shared the rooftop with Holmes. Knowing his abrupt mood swings, I moved slowly to brace myself against the chimney and prepared for any sudden impulses to which my friend might give in. How long we remained there, I know not, but my fears ultimately proved unfounded when I felt Holmes lay a weary hand on my shoulder.

"Come, Watson," he said. "Let's go inside."

We carefully retraced our steps and as we entered our

rooms, each immersed in his own thoughts, we both froze with surprise at the appearance of two gaily wrapped presents on the mantelpiece. A mutual nod was enough to send us moving quickly towards them, and a moment later Holmes stood with a new briar pipe and I with a new bowler hat. I could see that Holmes was greatly pleased, as was I, and I gingerly placed the bowler on my head. It fit perfectly.

"You know, Holmes," I began as I studied my profile in the mirror, "perhaps you shouldn't take your failure in this case quite so harshly."

"I daresay you're right, Watson," replied Holmes as he lit his new pipe with a twinkle in his eye. "Indeed, I'm beginning to think that some things best remain mysteries after all."

The End.